Russian Short Stories

RUSSIAN SHORT STORIES

LARGE PRINT EDITION

WWW.BIGFONTBOOKS.COM
ISBN-10:1-940849-49-7
ISBN-13:978-1-940849-49-2

Contents

INTRODUCTION 7
THE QUEEN OF SPADES 25
81
THE CLOAK 81
THE CHRISTMAS TREE AND THE WEDDING 139
THE DARLING 155
THE BET 181
VANKA 195
ONE AUTUMN NIGHT 203
HER LOVER 223
THE DISTRICT DOCTOR 235

INTRODUCTION

Conceive the joy of a lover of nature who, leaving the art galleries, wanders out among the trees and wild flowers and birds that the pictures of the galleries have sentimentalised. It is some such joy that the man who truly loves the noblest in letters feels when tasting for the first time the simple delights of Russian literature. French and English and German authors, too, occasionally, offer works of lofty, simple naturalness; but the very keynote to the whole of Russian literature is simplicity, naturalness, veraciousness.

Another essentially Russian trait is the quite unaffected conception that the lowly are on a plane of equality with the so-called upper classes. When the Englishman Dickens wrote with his profound pity and understanding of the poor, there was yet a bit; of remoteness, perhaps, even, a bit of caricature, in his treatment of them. He showed their sufferings to the rest of the world with a "Behold how the other half lives!" The Russian writes of the poor, as it were, from within, as one of them, with no eye to theatrical effect upon the well-to-do. There is no insistence upon peculiar virtues or vices. The poor are portrayed just as they are, as human beings like the rest of us. A democratic spirit is reflected, breathing a broad humanity, a true universality, an unstudied generosity that proceed not from the intellectual conviction that to understand all is to forgive all, but from an instinctive feeling that no man has the right to set himself up as a judge over another, that one can only observe and record.

In 1834 two short stories appeared, The Queen of Spades, by Pushkin, and The Cloak, by Gogol. The first was a finishing-off of the old, outgoing style of romanticism, the other was the beginning of the new, the characteristically Russian style. We read Pushkin's Queen of Spades, the first story in the volume, and the likelihood is we shall enjoy it greatly. "But why is it Russian?" we ask. The answer is, "It is not Russian." It might have been printed in an American magazine over the name of John Brown. But, now, take the very next story in the volume, The Cloak. "Ah," you exclaim, "a genuine Russian story, Surely. You cannot palm it off on me over the name of Jones or Smith." Why? Because The Cloak for the first time strikes that truly Russian note of deep sympathy with the disinherited. It is not yet wholly free from artificiality, and so is not yet typical of the purely realistic fiction that reached its perfected development in Turgenev and Tolstoy.

Though Pushkin heads the list of those writers who made the literature of their country world-famous, he was still a romanticist, in the universal literary fashion of his day. However, he already gave strong indication of the peculiarly Russian genius for naturalness or realism, and was a true Russian in his simplicity of style. In no sense an innovator, but taking the cue for his poetry from Byron and for his prose from the romanticism current at that period, he was not in advance of his age. He had a revolutionary streak in his nature, as his Ode to Liberty and other bits of verse and his intimacy with the Decembrist rebels show. But his youthful fire soon died down, and he found it possible to accommodate himself to the life of a Russian high functionary and courtier under the severe despot Nicholas

I, though, to be sure, he always hated that life. For all his flirting with revolutionarism, he never displayed great originality or depth of thought. He was simply an extraordinarily gifted author, a perfect versifier, a wondrous lyrist, and a delicious raconteur, endowed with a grace, ease and power of expression that delighted even the exacting artistic sense of Turgenev. To him aptly applies the dictum of Socrates: "Not by wisdom do the poets write poetry, but by a sort of genius and inspiration." I do not mean to convey that as a thinker Pushkin is to be despised. Nevertheless, it is true that he would occupy a lower position in literature did his reputation depend upon his contributions to thought and not upon his value as an artist.

"We are all descended from Gogol's Cloak," said a Russian writer. And Dostoyevsky's novel, Poor People, which appeared ten years later, is, in a way, merely an extension of Gogol's shorter tale. In Dostoyevsky, indeed, the passion for the common people and the all-embracing, all-penetrating pity for suffering humanity reach their climax. He was a profound psychologist and delved deeply into the human soul, especially in its abnormal and diseased aspects. Between scenes of heart-rending, abject poverty, injustice, and wrong, and the torments of mental pathology, he managed almost to exhaust the whole range of human woe. And he analysed this misery with an intensity of feeling and a painstaking regard for the most harrowing details that are quite upsetting to normally constituted nerves. Yet all the horrors must be forgiven him because of the motive inspiring them—an overpowering love and the desire to induce an equal love in others. It is not horror for horror's sake, not a literary tour de force, as in Poe, but horror for a high purpose, for purification through suffering, which was one of the articles of Dostoyevsky's faith.

Following as a corollary from the love and pity for mankind that make a leading element in Russian literature, is a passionate search for the means of improving the lot of humanity, a fervent attachment to social ideas and ideals. A Russian author is more ardently devoted to a cause than an American short-story writer to a plot. This, in turn, is but a reflection of the spirit of the Russian people, especially of the intellectuals. The Russians take literature perhaps more seriously than any other nation. To them books are not a mere diversion. They demand that fiction and poetry be a true mirror of life and be of service to life. A Russian author, to achieve the highest recognition, must be a thinker also. He need not necessarily be a finished artist. Everything is subordinated to two main requirements—humanitarian ideals and fidelity to life. This is the secret of the marvellous simplicity of Russian-literary art. Before the supreme function of literature, the Russian writer stands awed and humbled. He knows he cannot cover up poverty of thought, poverty of spirit and lack of sincerity by rhetorical tricks or verbal cleverness. And if he possesses the two essential requirements, the simplest language will suffice.

These qualities are exemplified at their best by Turgenev and Tolstoy. They both had a strong social consciousness; they both grappled with the problems of human welfare; they were both artists in the larger sense, that is, in their truthful representation of life, Turgenev was an artist also in the narrower sense—in a keen appreciation Of form. Thoroughly Occidental in his tastes, he sought the regeneration of Russia in radical progress along the lines of European democracy. Tolstoy, on the other hand, sought the salvation of mankind in a return to the primitive life and primitive

Christian religion.

The very first work of importance by Turgenev, A Sportsman's Sketches, dealt with the question of serfdom, and it wielded tremendous influence in bringing about its abolition. Almost every succeeding book of his, from Rudin through Fathers and Sons to Virgin Soil, presented vivid pictures of contemporary Russian society, with its problems, the clash of ideas between the old and the new generations, and the struggles, the aspirations and the thoughts that engrossed the advanced youth of Russia; so that his collected works form a remarkable literary record of the successive movements of Russian society in a period of preparation, fraught with epochal significance, which culminated in the overthrow of Czarism and the inauguration of a new and true democracy, marking the beginning, perhaps, of a radical transformation the world over.

"The greatest writer of Russia." That is Turgenev's estimate of Tolstoy. "A second Shakespeare!" was Flaubert's enthusiastic outburst. The Frenchman's comparison is not wholly illuminating. The one point of resemblance between the two authors is simply in the tremendous magnitude of their genius. Each is a Colossus. Each creates a whole world of characters, from kings and princes and ladies to servants and maids and peasants. But how vastly divergent the angle of approach! Anna Karenina may have all the subtle womanly charm of an Olivia or a Portia, but how different her trials. Shakespeare could not have treated Anna's problems at all. Anna could not have appeared in his pages except as a sinning Gertrude, the mother of Hamlet. Shakespeare had all the prejudices of his age. He accepted the world as it is with its absurd moralities, its conventions and institutions and social classes. A gravedigger is naturally inferior to a lord, and if he is to be presented at all, he must come on as a clown. The people are always a mob, the rabble. Tolstoy, is the revolutionist, the iconoclast. He has the completest independence of mind. He utterly refuses to accept established opinions just because they are established. He probes into the right and wrong of things. His is a broad, generous universal democracy, his is a comprehensive sympathy, his an absolute incapacity to evaluate human beings according to station, rank or profession, or any standard but that of spiritual worth. In all this he was a complete contrast to Shakespeare. Each of the two men was like a creature of a higher world, possessed of supernatural endowments. Their omniscience of all things human, their insight into the hiddenmost springs of men's actions appear miraculous. But Shakespeare makes the impression of detachment from his works. The works do not reveal the man; while in Tolstoy the greatness of the man blends with the greatness of the genius. Tolstoy was no mere oracle uttering profundities he wot not of. As the social, religious and moral tracts that he wrote in the latter period of his life are instinct with a literary beauty of which he never could divest himself, and which gave an artistic value even to his sermons, so his earlier novels show a profound concern for the welfare of society, a broad, humanitarian spirit, a bigness of soul that included prince and pauper alike.

Is this extravagant praise? Then let me echo William Dean Howells: "I know very well that I do not speak of Tolstoy's books in measured terms; I cannot."

The Russian writers so far considered have made valuable contributions to the short story; but, with the exception of Pushkin, whose reputation rests chiefly upon his poetry, their best work, generally, was in the field of the long novel. It was the novel that gave Russian literature its pre-eminence. It could not have been otherwise, since Russia is young as a literary nation, and did not come of age until the period at which the novel was almost the only form of literature that counted. If, therefore, Russia was to gain distinction in the world of letters, it could be only through the novel. Of the measure of her success there is perhaps no better testimony than the words of Matthew Arnold, a critic certainly not given to overstatement. "The Russian novel," he wrote in 1887, "has now the vogue, and deserves to have it… The Russian novelist is master of a spell to which the secret of human nature—both what is external and internal, gesture and manner no less than thought and feeling—willingly make themselves known… In that form of imaginative literature, which in our day is the most popular and the most possible, the Russians at the present moment seem to me to hold the field."

With the strict censorship imposed on Russian writers, many of them who might perhaps have contented themselves with expressing their opinions in essays, were driven to conceal their meaning under the guise of satire or allegory; which gave rise to a peculiar genre of literature, a sort of editorial or essay done into fiction, in which the satirist Saltykov, a contemporary of Turgenev and Dostoyevsky, who wrote under the pseudonym of Shchedrin, achieved the greatest success and popularity.

It was not however, until the concluding quarter of the last century that writers like Korolenko and Garshin arose, who devoted themselves chiefly to the cultivation of the short story. With Anton Chekhov the short story assumed a position of importance alongside the larger works of the great Russian masters. Gorky and Andreyev made the short story do the same service for the active revolutionary period in the last decade of the nineteenth century down to its temporary defeat in 1906 that Turgenev rendered in his series of larger novels for the period of preparation. But very different was the voice of Gorky, the man sprung from the people, the embodiment of all the accumulated wrath and indignation of centuries of social wrong and oppression, from the gentlemanly tones of the cultured artist Turgenev. Like a mighty hammer his blows fell upon the decaying fabric of the old society. His was no longer a feeble, despairing protest. With the strength and confidence of victory he made onslaught upon onslaught on the old institutions until they shook and almost tumbled. And when reaction celebrated its short-lived triumph and gloom settled again upon his country and most of his co-fighters withdrew from the battle in despair, some returning to the old-time Russian mood of hopelessness, passivity and apathy, and some even backsliding into wild orgies of literary debauchery, Gorky never wavered, never lost his faith and hope, never for a moment was untrue to his principles. Now, with the revolution victorious, he has come into his right, one of the most respected, beloved and picturesque figures in the Russian democracy.

Kuprin, the most facile and talented short-story writer next to Chekhov, has, on the whole, kept well to the best literary traditions of Russia, though he has frequently wandered off to extravagant sex themes, for which he seems to display as great a fondness as Artzybashev. Semyonov is a unique character in Russian literature, a peasant who had scarcely mastered the most elementary mechanics of writing when he penned his first story. But that story pleased Tolstoy, who befriended and encouraged him. His tales deal altogether with peasant life in country and city, and have a lifelikeness, an artlessness, a simplicity striking even in a Russian author.

There is a small group of writers detached from the main current of

Russian literature who worship at the shrine of beauty and mysticism.

Of these Sologub has attained the highest reputation.

Rich as Russia has become in the short story, Anton Chekhov still stands out as the supreme master, one of the greatest short-story writers of the world. He was born in Taganarok, in the Ukraine, in 1860, the son of a peasant serf who succeeded in buying his freedom. Anton Chekhov studied medicine, but devoted himself largely to writing, in which, he acknowledged, his scientific training was of great service. Though he lived only forty-four years, dying of tuberculosis in 1904, his collected works consist of sixteen fair-sized volumes of short stories, and several dramas besides. A few volumes of his works have already appeared in English translation.

Critics, among them Tolstoy, have often compared Chekhov to Maupassant. I find it hard to discover the resemblance. Maupassant holds a supreme position as a short-story writer; so does Chekhov. But there, it seems to me, the likeness ends.

The chill wind that blows from the atmosphere created by the Frenchman's objective artistry is by the Russian commingled with the warm breath of a great human sympathy. Maupassant never tells where his sympathies lie, and you don't know; you only guess. Chekhov does not tell you where his sympathies lie, either, but you know all the same; you don't have to guess. And yet Chekhov is as objective as Maupassant. In the chronicling of facts, conditions, and situations, in the reproduction of characters, he is scrupulously true, hard, and inexorable. But without obtruding his personality, he somehow manages to let you know that he is always present, always at hand. If you laugh, he is there to laugh with you; if you cry, he is there to shed a tear with you; if you are horrified, he is horrified, too. It is a subtle art by which he contrives to make one feel the nearness of himself for all his objectiveness, so subtle that it defies analysis. And yet it constitutes one of the great charms of his tales.

Chekhov's works show an astounding resourcefulness and versatility. There is no monotony, no repetition. Neither in incident nor in character are any two stories alike. The range of Chekhov's knowledge of men and things seems to be unlimited, and he is extravagant in the use of it. Some great idea which many a writer would consider sufficient to expand into a whole novel he disposes of in a story of a few pages. Take, for example, Vanka, apparently but a mere episode in the childhood of a nine-year-old boy; while it is really the tragedy of a whole life in its tempting glimpses into a past environment and ominous forebodings of the future—all contracted into the space of four or five pages. Chekhov is lavish with his inventiveness. Apparently, it cost him no effort to invent.

I have used the word inventiveness for lack of a better name. It expresses but lamely the peculiar faculty that distinguishes Chekhov. Chekhov does not really invent. He reveals. He reveals things that no author before him has revealed. It is as though he possessed a special organ which enabled him to see, hear and feel things of which we other mortals did not even dream the existence. Yet when he lays them bare we know that they are not fictitious, not invented, but as real as the ordinary familiar facts of life. This faculty of his playing on all conceivable objects, all conceivable emotions, no matter how microscopic, endows them with life and a soul. By virtue of this power The Steppe, an uneventful record of peasants travelling day after day through flat, monotonous fields, becomes instinct with dramatic interest, and its 125 pages seem all too short. And by virtue of the same attribute we follow with breathless suspense the minute description of the declining days of a great scientist, who feels his physical and mental faculties gradually ebbing away. A Tiresome Story, Chekhov calls it; and so it would be without the vitality conjured into it by the magic touch of this strange genius.

Divination is perhaps a better term than invention. Chekhov divines the most secret impulses of the soul, scents out what is buried in the subconscious, and brings it up to the surface. Most writers are specialists. They know certain strata of society, and when they venture beyond, their step becomes uncertain. Chekhov's material is only delimited by humanity. He is equally at home everywhere. The peasant, the labourer, the merchant, the priest, the professional man, the scholar, the military officer, and the government functionary, Gentile or Jew, man, woman, or child—Chekhov is intimate with all of them. His characters are sharply defined individuals, not types. In almost all his stories, however short, the men and women and children who play a part in them come out as clear, distinct personalities. Ariadne is as vivid a character as Lilly, the heroine of Sudermann's Song of Songs; yet Ariadne is but a single story in a volume of stories. Who that has read The Darling can ever forget her—the woman who had no separate existence of her own, but thought the thoughts, felt the feelings, and spoke the words of the men she loved? And when there was no man to love any more, she was utterly crushed until she found a child to take care of and to love; and then she sank her personality in the boy as she had sunk it before in her husbands and lover, became a mere reflection of him, and was happy again.

In the compilation of this volume I have been guided by the desire to give the largest possible representation to the prominent authors of the Russian short story, and to present specimens characteristic of each. At the same time the element of interest has been kept in mind; and in a few instances, as in the case of Korolenko, the selection of the story was made with a view to its intrinsic merit and striking qualities rather than as typifying the writer's art. It was, of course, impossible in the space of one book to exhaust all that is best. But to my knowledge, the present volume is the most comprehensive anthology of the Russian short story in the English language, and gives a fair notion of the achievement in that field. All who enjoy good reading, I have no reason to doubt, will get pleasure from it, and if, in addition, it will prove of assistance to American students of Russian literature, I shall feel that the task has been doubly worth the while.

Korolenko's Shades and Andreyev's Lazarus first appeared in Current Opinion, and Artzybashev's The Revolutionist in the Metropolitan Magazine. I take pleasure in thanking Mr. Edward J. Wheeler, editor of Current Opinion, and Mr. Carl Hovey, editor of the Metropolitan Magazine, for permission to reprint them.

THE QUEEN OF SPADES

BY ALEXSANDR S. PUSHKIN

I

There was a card party at the rooms of Narumov of the Horse Guards. The long winter night passed away imperceptibly, and it was five o'clock in the morning before the company sat down to supper. Those who had won, ate with a good appetite; the others sat staring absently at their empty plates. When the champagne appeared, however, the conversation became more animated, and all took a part in it.

"And how did you fare, Surin?" asked the host.

"Oh, I lost, as usual. I must confess that I

am unlucky: I play mirandole, I always keep cool, I never allow anything to put me out, and yet I always lose!"

"And you did not once allow yourself to be tempted to back the red?...

Your firmness astonishes me."

"But what do you think of Hermann?" said one of the guests, pointing to a young Engineer: "he has never had a card in his hand in his life, he has never in his life laid a wager, and yet he sits here till five o'clock in the morning watching our play."

"Play interests me very much," said Hermann: "but I am not in the position to sacrifice the necessary in the hope of winning the superfluous."

"Hermann is a German: he is economical—that is all!" observed Tomsky. "But if there is one person that I cannot understand, it is my grandmother, the Countess Anna Fedotovna."

"How so?" inquired the guests.

"I cannot understand," continued Tomsky, "how it is that my grandmother does not punt."

"What is there remarkable about an old lady of eighty not punting?" said Narumov.

"Then you do not know the reason why?"

"No, really; haven't the faintest idea."

"Oh! then listen. About sixty years ago, my grandmother went to Paris, where she created quite a sensation. People used to run after her to catch a glimpse of the 'Muscovite Venus.' Richelieu made love to her, and my grandmother maintains that he almost blew out his brains in consequence of her cruelty. At that time ladies used to play at faro. On one occasion at the Court, she lost a very considerable sum to the Duke of Orleans. On returning home, my grandmother removed the patches from her face, took off her hoops, informed my grandfather of her loss at the gaming-table, and ordered him to pay the money. My deceased grandfather, as far as I remember, was a sort of house-steward to my grandmother. He dreaded her like fire; but, on hearing of such a heavy loss, he almost went out of his mind; he calculated the various sums she had lost, and pointed out to her that in six months she had spent half a million francs, that neither their Moscow nor Saratov estates were in Paris, and finally refused point blank to pay the debt. My grandmother gave him a box on the ear and slept by herself as a sign of her displeasure. The next day she sent for her husband, hoping that this domestic punishment had produced an effect upon him, but she found him inflexible. For the first time in her life, she entered into reasonings and explanations with him, thinking to be able to convince him by pointing out to him that there are debts and debts, and that there is a great difference between a Prince and a coachmaker. But it was all in vain, my grandfather still remained obdurate. But the matter did not rest there. My grandmother did not know what to do. She had shortly before become acquainted with a very remarkable man. You have heard of Count St. Germain, about whom so many marvellous stories are told. You know that he represented himself as the Wandering Jew, as the discoverer of the elixir of life, of the philosopher's stone, and so forth. Some laughed at him as a charlatan; but Casanova, in his memoirs, says that he was a spy. But be that as it may, St. Germain, in spite of the mystery surrounding him, was a very fascinating person, and was much sought after in the best circles of society. Even to this day my grandmother retains an affectionate recollection of him, and becomes quite angry if any one speaks disrespectfully of him. My grandmother knew that St. Germain had large sums of money at his disposal. She resolved to have recourse to him, and she wrote a letter to him asking him to come to her without delay. The queer old man immediately waited upon her and found her overwhelmed with grief. She described to him in the blackest colours the barbarity of her husband, and ended by declaring that her whole hope depended upon his friendship and amiability.

"St. Germain reflected.

"'I could advance you the sum you want,' said he; 'but I know that you would not rest easy until you had paid me back, and I should not like to bring fresh troubles upon you. But there is another way of getting out of your difficulty: you can win back your money.'

"'But, my dear Count,' replied my grandmother, 'I tell you that I haven't any money left.'

"'Money is not necessary,' replied St. Germain: 'be pleased to listen to me.'

"Then he revealed to her a secret, for which each of us would give a good deal..."

The young officers listened with increased attention. Tomsky lit his pipe, puffed away for a moment and then continued:

"That same evening my grandmother went to Versailles to the jeu de la reine. The Duke of Orleans kept the bank; my grandmother excused herself in an off-hand manner for not having yet paid her debt, by inventing some little story, and then began to play against him. She chose three cards and played them one after the other: all three won sonika, [Said of a card when it wins or loses in the quickest possible time.] and my grandmother recovered every farthing that she had lost."

"Mere chance!" said one of the guests.

"A tale!" observed Hermann.

"Perhaps they were marked cards!" said a third.

"I do not think so," replied Tomsky gravely.

"What!" said Narumov, "you have a grandmother who knows how to hit upon three lucky cards in succession, and you have never yet succeeded in getting the secret of it out of her?"

"That's the deuce of it!" replied Tomsky: "she had four sons, one of whom was my father; all four were determined gamblers, and yet not to one of them did she ever reveal her secret, although it would not have been a bad thing either for them or for me. But this is what I heard from my uncle, Count Ivan Ilyich, and he assured me, on his honour, that it was true. The late Chaplitzky—the same who died in poverty after having squandered millions—once lost, in his youth, about three hundred thousand roubles—to Zorich, if I remember rightly. He was in despair. My grandmother, who was always very severe upon the extravagance of young men, took pity, however, upon Chaplitzky. She gave him three cards, telling him to play them one after the other, at the same time exacting from him a solemn promise that he would never play at cards again as long as he lived. Chaplitzky then went to his victorious opponent, and they began a fresh game. On the first card he staked fifty thousand rubles and won sonika;

he doubled the stake and won again, till at last, by pursuing the same tactics, he won back more than he had lost …

"But it is time to go to bed: it is a quarter to six already."

And indeed it was already beginning to dawn: the young men emptied their glasses and then took leave of each other.

II

The old Countess A—— was seated in her dressing-room in front of her looking—glass. Three waiting maids stood around her. One held a small pot of rouge, another a box of hair-pins, and the third a tall can with bright red ribbons. The Countess had no longer the slightest pretensions to beauty, but she still preserved the habits of her youth, dressed in strict accordance with the fashion of seventy years before, and made as long and as careful a toilette as she would have done sixty years previously. Near the window, at an embroidery frame, sat a young lady, her ward.

"Good morning, grandmamma," said a young officer, entering the room. "Bonjour,

Mademoiselle Lise. Grandmamma, I want to ask you something."

"What is it, Paul?"

"I want you to let me introduce one of my friends to you, and to allow me to bring him to the ball on Friday."

"Bring him direct to the ball and introduce him to me there. Were you at B——'s yesterday?"

"Yes; everything went off very pleasantly, and dancing was kept up until five o'clock. How charming Yeletzkaya was!"

"But, my dear, what is there charming about her? Isn't she like her grandmother, the Princess Daria Petrovna? By the way, she must be very old, the Princess Daria Petrovna."

"How do you mean, old?" cried Tomsky thoughtlessly; "she died seven years ago."

The young lady raised her head and made a sign to the young officer. He then remembered that the old Countess was never to be informed of the death of any of her contemporaries, and he bit his lips. But the old Countess heard the news with the greatest indifference.

"Dead!" said she; "and I did not know it. We were appointed maids of honour at the same time, and when we were presented to the Empress…"

And the Countess for the hundredth time related to her grandson one of her anecdotes.

"Come, Paul," said she, when she had finished her story, "help me to get up. Lizanka, where is my snuff-box?"

And the Countess with her three maids went behind a screen to finish her toilette. Tomsky was left alone with the young lady.

"Who is the gentleman you wish to introduce to the Countess?" asked
Lizaveta Ivanovna in a whisper.
"Narumov. Do you know him?"

"No. Is he a soldier or a civilian?"

"A soldier."

“Is he in the Engineers?”

“No, in the Cavalry. What made you think that he was in the
Engineers?”
The young lady smiled, but made no reply.

“Paul,” cried the Countess from behind the screen, “send me some new novel, only pray don’t let it be one of the present day style.”

“What do you mean, grandmother?”

“That is, a novel, in which the hero strangles neither his father nor his mother, and in which there are no drowned bodies. I have a great horror of drowned persons.”

“There are no such novels nowadays. Would you like a Russian one?”

“Are there any Russian novels? Send me one, my dear, pray send me one!”

“Good-bye, grandmother: I am in a hurry... Good-bye, Lizaveta
Ivanovna. What made you think that Narumov was in the Engineers?”
And Tomsky left the boudoir.

Lizaveta Ivanovna was left alone: she laid aside her work and began to look out of the window. A few moments afterwards, at a corner house on the other side of the street, a young officer appeared. A deep blush covered her cheeks; she took up her work again and bent her head down over the frame. At the same moment the Countess returned completely dressed.

"Order the carriage, Lizaveta," said she; "we will go out for a drive."

Lizaveta arose from the frame and began to arrange her work.

"What is the matter with you, my child, are you deaf?" cried the

Countess. "Order the carriage to be got ready at once."

"I will do so this moment," replied the young lady, hastening into the ante-room.

A servant entered and gave the Countess some books from Prince Paul

Aleksandrovich.

"Tell him that I am much obliged to him," said the Countess.

"Lizaveta! Lizaveta! Where are you running to?"

"I am going to dress."

"There is plenty of time, my dear. Sit down here. Open the first volume and read to me aloud."

Her companion took the book and read a few lines.

"Louder," said the Countess. "What is the matter with you, my child? Have you lost your voice? Wait—give me that footstool—a little nearer—that will do."

Lizaveta read two more pages. The Countess yawned.

"Put the book down," said she: "what a lot of nonsense! Send it back to Prince Paul with my thanks... But where is the carriage?"

"The carriage is ready," said Lizaveta, looking out into the street.

"How is it that you are not dressed?" said the Countess: "I must always wait for you. It is intolerable, my dear!"

Liza hastened to her room. She had not been there two minutes, before the Countess began to ring with all her might. The three waiting-maids came running in at one door and the valet at another.

"How is it that you cannot hear me when I ring for you?" said the

Countess. "Tell Lizaveta Ivanovna that I am waiting for her."

Lizaveta returned with her hat and cloak on.

"At last you are here!" said the Countess. "But why such an elaborate toilette? Whom do you intend to captivate? What sort of weather is it? It seems rather windy."

"No, your Ladyship, it is very calm," replied the valet.

"You never think of what you are talking about. Open the window. So it is: windy and bitterly cold. Unharness the horses. Lizaveta, we won't go out—there was no need for you to deck yourself like that."

"What a life is mine!" thought Lizaveta Ivanovna.

And, in truth, Lizaveta Ivanovna was a very unfortunate creature. “The bread of the stranger is bitter,” says Dante, “and his staircase hard to climb.” But who can know what the bitterness of dependence is so well as the poor companion of an old lady of quality? The Countess A—— had by no means a bad heart, but she was capricious, like a woman who had been spoilt by the world, as well as being avaricious and egotistical, like all old people who have seen their best days, and whose thoughts are with the past and not the present. She participated in all the vanities of the great world, went to balls, where she sat in a corner, painted and dressed in old-fashioned style, like a deformed but indispensable ornament of the ball-room; all the guests on entering approached her and made a profound bow, as if in accordance with a set ceremony, but after that nobody took any further notice of her. She received the whole town at her house, and observed the strictest etiquette, although she could no longer recognise the faces of people. Her numerous domestics, growing fat and old in her ante-chamber and servants’ hall, did just as they liked, and vied with each other in robbing the aged Countess in the most bare-faced manner. Lizaveta Ivanovna was the martyr of the household. She made tea, and was reproached with using too much sugar; she read novels aloud to the Countess, and the faults of the author were visited upon her head; she accompanied the Countess in her walks, and was held answerable for the weather or the state of the pavement. A salary was attached to the post, but she very rarely received it, although she was expected to dress like everybody else, that is to say, like very few indeed. In society she played the most pitiable role. Everybody knew her, and nobody paid her any attention. At balls she danced only when a partner was wanted, and ladies would only take hold of her arm when it was necessary to lead her out of the room to attend to their dresses. She was very self-conscious, and felt her position keenly, and she looked about her with impatience for a deliverer to come to her rescue; but the young men, calculating in their giddiness, honoured her with but very little attention, although Lizaveta Ivanovna was a hundred times prettier than the bare-faced and cold-hearted marriageable girls around whom they hovered. Many a time did she quietly slink away from the glittering but wearisome drawing-room, to go and cry in her own poor little room, in which stood a screen, a chest of drawers, a looking-glass and a painted bedstead, and where a tallow candle burnt feebly in a copper candle-stick.

One morning—this was about two days after the evening party described at the beginning of this story, and a week previous to the scene at which we have just assisted—Lizaveta Ivanovna was seated near the window at her embroidery frame, when, happening to look out into the street, she caught sight of a young Engineer officer, standing motionless with his eyes fixed upon her window. She lowered her head and went on again with her work. About five minutes afterwards she looked out again—the young officer was still standing in the same place. Not being in the habit of coquetting with passing officers, she did not continue to gaze out into the street, but went on sewing for a couple of hours, without raising her head. Dinner was announced. She rose up and began to put her embroidery away, but glancing casually out of the window, she perceived the officer again. This seemed to her very strange. After dinner she went to the window with a certain feeling of uneasiness, but the officer was no longer there—and she thought no more about him.

A couple of days afterwards, just as she was stepping into the carriage with the Countess, she saw him again. He was standing close behind the door, with his face half-concealed by his fur collar, but his dark eyes sparkled beneath his cap. Lizaveta felt alarmed, though she knew not why, and she trembled as she seated herself in the carriage.

On returning home, she hastened to the window—the officer was standing in his accustomed place, with his eyes fixed upon her. She drew back, a prey to curiosity and agitated by a feeling which was quite new to her.

From that time forward not a day passed without the young officer making his appearance under the window at the customary hour, and between him and her there was established a sort of mute acquaintance. Sitting in her place at work, she used to feel his approach; and raising her head, she would look at him longer and longer each day. The young man seemed to be very grateful to her: she saw with the sharp eye of youth, how a sudden flush covered his pale cheeks each time that their glances met. After about a week she commenced to smile at him...

When Tomsky asked permission of his grandmother the Countess to present one of his friends to her, the young girl's heart beat violently. But hearing that Narumov was not an Engineer, she regretted that by her thoughtless question, she had betrayed her secret to the volatile Tomsky.

Hermann was the son of a German who had become a naturalised Russian, and from whom he had inherited a small capital. Being firmly convinced of the necessity of preserving his independence, Hermann did not touch his private income, but lived on his pay, without allowing himself the slightest luxury. Moreover, he was reserved and ambitious, and his companions rarely had an opportunity of making merry at the expense of his extreme parsimony. He had strong passions and an ardent imagination, but his firmness of disposition preserved him from the ordinary errors of young men. Thus, though a gamester at heart, he never touched a card, for he considered his position did not allow him—as he said—"to risk the necessary in the hope of winning the superfluous," yet he would sit for nights together at the card table and follow with feverish anxiety the different turns of the game.

The story of the three cards had produced a powerful impression upon his imagination, and all night long he could think of nothing else. "If," he thought to himself the following evening, as he walked along the streets of St. Petersburg, "if the old Countess would but reveal her secret to me! if she would only tell me the names of the three winning cards. Why should I not try my fortune? I must get introduced to her and win her favour—become her lover... But all that will take time, and she is eighty-seven years old: she might be dead in a week, in a couple of days even!... But the story itself: can it really be true?... No! Economy, temperance and industry: those are my three winning cards; by means of them I shall be able to double my capital—increase it sevenfold, and procure for myself ease and independence."

Musing in this manner, he walked on until he found himself in one of the principal streets of St. Petersburg, in front of a house of antiquated architecture. The street was blocked with equipages; carriages one after the other drew up in front of the brilliantly illuminated doorway. At one moment there stepped out on to the pavement the well-shaped little foot of some young beauty, at another the heavy boot of a cavalry officer, and then the silk stockings and shoes of a member of the diplomatic world. Furs and cloaks passed in rapid succession before the gigantic porter at the entrance.

Hermann stopped. "Whose house is this?" he asked of the watchman at the corner.

"The Countess A——'s," replied the watchman.

Hermann started. The strange story of the three cards again presented itself to his imagination. He began walking up and down before the house, thinking of its owner and her strange secret. Returning late to his modest lodging, he could not go to sleep for a long time, and when at last he did doze off, he could dream of nothing but cards, green tables, piles of banknotes and heaps of ducats. He played one card after the other, winning uninterruptedly, and then he gathered up the gold and filled his pockets with the notes. When he woke up late the next morning, he sighed over the loss of his imaginary wealth, and then sallying out into the town, he found himself once more in front of the Countess's residence. Some unknown power seemed to have attracted him thither. He stopped and looked up at the windows. At one of these he saw a head with luxuriant black hair, which was bent down probably over some book or an embroidery frame. The head was raised. Hermann saw a fresh complexion and a pair of dark eyes. That moment decided his fate.

III

Lizaveta Ivanovna had scarcely taken off her hat and cloak, when the Countess sent for her and again ordered her to get the carriage ready. The vehicle drew up before the door, and they prepared to take their seats. Just at the moment when two footmen were assisting the old lady to enter the carriage, Lizaveta saw her Engineer standing close beside the wheel; he grasped her hand; alarm caused her to lose her presence of mind, and the young man disappeared—but not before he had left a letter between her fingers. She concealed it in her glove, and during the whole of the drive she neither saw nor heard anything. It was the custom of the Countess, when out for an airing in her carriage, to be constantly asking such questions as: "Who was that person that met us just now? What is the name of this bridge? What is written on that signboard?" On this occasion, however, Lizaveta returned such vague and absurd answers, that the Countess became angry with her.

"What is the matter with you, my dear?" she exclaimed. "Have you taken leave of your senses, or what is it? Do you not hear me or understand what I say?... Heaven be thanked, I am still in my right mind and speak plainly enough!"

Lizaveta Ivanovna did not hear her. On returning home she ran to her room, and drew the letter out of her glove: it was not sealed. Lizaveta read it. The letter contained a declaration of love; it was tender, respectful, and copied word for word from a German novel. But Lizaveta did not know anything of the German language, and she was quite delighted.

For all that, the letter caused her to feel exceedingly uneasy. For the first time in her life she was entering into secret and confidential relations with a young man. His boldness alarmed her. She reproached herself for her imprudent behaviour, and knew not what to do. Should she cease to sit at the window and, by assuming an appearance of indifference towards him, put a check upon the young officer's desire for further acquaintance with her? Should she send his letter back to him, or should she answer him in a cold and decided manner? There was nobody to whom she could turn in her perplexity, for she had neither female friend nor adviser… At length she resolved to reply to him.

She sat down at her little writing-table, took pen and paper, and began to think. Several times she began her letter, and then tore it up: the way she had expressed herself seemed to her either too inviting or too cold and decisive. At last she succeeded in writing a few lines with which she felt satisfied.

"I am convinced," she wrote, "that your intentions are honourable, and that you do not wish to offend me by any imprudent behaviour, but our acquaintance must not begin in such a manner. I return you your letter, and I hope that I shall never have any cause to complain of this undeserved slight."

The next day, as soon as Hermann made his appearance, Lizaveta rose from her embroidery, went into the drawing-room, opened the ventilator and threw the letter into the street, trusting that the young officer would have the perception to pick it up.

Hermann hastened forward, picked it up and then repaired to a confectioner's shop. Breaking the seal of the envelope, he found inside it his own letter and Lizaveta's reply. He had expected this, and he returned home, his mind deeply oc cupied with his intrigue.

Three days afterwards, a bright-eyed young girl from a milliner's establishment brought Lizaveta a letter. Lizaveta opened it with great uneasiness, fearing that it was a demand for money, when suddenly she recognised Hermann's hand-writing.

"You have made a mistake, my dear," said she: "this letter is not for me."

"Oh, yes, it is for you," replied the girl, smiling very knowingly.

"Have the goodness to read it."

Lizaveta glanced at the letter. Hermann

requested an interview.

"It cannot be," she cried, alarmed at the audacious request, and the manner in which it was made. "This letter is certainly not for me."

And she tore it into fragments.

"If the letter was not for you, why have you torn it up?" said the girl. "I should have given it back to the person who sent it."

"Be good enough, my dear," said Lizaveta, disconcerted by this remark, "not to bring me any more letters for the future, and tell the person who sent you that he ought to be ashamed..."

But Hermann was not the man to be thus put off. Every day Lizaveta received from him a letter, sent now in this way, now in that. They were no longer translated from the German. Hermann wrote them under the inspiration of passion, and spoke in his own language, and they bore full testimony to the inflexibility of his desire and the disordered condition of his uncontrollable imagination. Lizaveta no longer thought of sending them back to him: she became intoxicated with them and began to reply to them, and little by little her answers became longer and more affectionate. At last she threw out of the window to him the following letter:

"This evening there is going to be a ball at the Embassy. The Countess will be there. We shall remain until two o'clock. You have now an opportunity of seeing me alone. As soon as the Countess is gone, the servants will very probably go out, and there will be nobody left but the Swiss, but he usually goes to sleep in his lodge. Come about half-past eleven. Walk straight upstairs. If you meet anybody in the ante-room, ask if the Countess is at home. You will be told 'No,' in which case there will be nothing left for you to do but to go away again. But it is most probable that you will meet nobody. The maidservants will all be together in one room. On leaving the ante-room, turn to the left, and walk straight on until you reach the Countess's bedroom. In the bedroom, behind a screen, you will find two doors: the one on the right leads to a cabinet, which the Countess never enters; the one on the left leads to a corridor, at the end of which is a little winding staircase; this leads to my room."

Hermann trembled like a tiger, as he waited

for the appointed time to arrive. At ten o'clock in the evening he was already in front of the Countess's house. The weather was terrible; the wind blew with great violence; the sleety snow fell in large flakes; the lamps emitted a feeble light, the streets were deserted; from time to time a sledge, drawn by a sorry-looking hack, passed by, on the look-out for a belated passenger. Hermann was enveloped in a thick overcoat, and felt neither wind nor snow.

At last the Countess's carriage drew up. Hermann saw two footmen carry out in their arms the bent form of the old lady, wrapped in sable fur, and immediately behind her, clad in a warm mantle, and with her head ornamented with a wreath of fresh flowers, followed Lizaveta. The door was closed. The carriage rolled away heavily through the yielding snow. The porter shut the street-door; the windows became dark.

Hermann began walking up and down near the deserted house; at length he stopped under a lamp, and glanced at his watch: it was twenty minutes past eleven. He remained standing under the lamp, his eyes fixed upon the watch, impatiently waiting for the remaining minutes to pass. At half-past eleven precisely, Hermann ascended the steps of the house, and made his way into the brightly-illuminated vestibule. The porter was not there. Hermann hastily ascended the staircase, opened the door of the ante-room and saw a footman sitting asleep in an antique chair by the side of a lamp. With a light firm step Hermann passed by him. The drawing-room and dining-room were in darkness, but a feeble reflection penetrated thither from the lamp in the ante-room.

Hermann reached the Countess's bedroom. Before a shrine, which was full of old images, a golden lamp was burning. Faded stuffed chairs and divans with soft cushions stood in melancholy symmetry around the room, the walls of which were hung with China silk. On one side of the room hung two portraits painted in Paris by Madame Lebrun. One of these represented a stout, red-faced man of about forty years of age in a bright-green uniform and with a star upon his breast; the other—a beautiful young woman, with an aquiline nose, forehead curls and a rose in her powdered hair. In the corners stood porcelain shepherds and shepherdesses, dining-room clocks from the workshop of the celebrated Lefroy, bandboxes, roulettes, fans and the various playthings for the amusement of ladies that were in vogue at the end of the last century, when Montgolfier's balloons and Mesmer's magnetism were the rage. Hermann stepped behind the screen. At the back of it stood a little iron bedstead; on the right was the door which led to the cabinet; on the left—the other which led to the corridor. He opened the latter, and saw the little winding staircase which led to the room of the poor companion... But he retraced his steps and entered the dark cabinet.

The time passed slowly. All was still. The clock in the drawing-room struck twelve; the strokes echoed through the room one after the other, and everything was quiet again. Hermann stood leaning against the cold stove. He was calm; his heart beat regularly, like that of a man resolved upon a dangerous but inevitable undertaking. One o'clock in the morning struck; then two; and he heard the distant noise of carriage-wheels. An involuntary agitation took possession of him. The carriage drew near and stopped. He heard the sound of the carriage-steps being let down. All was bustle within the house. The servants were running hither and thither, there was a confusion of voices, and the rooms were lit up. Three antiquated chamber-maids entered the bedroom, and they were shortly afterwards followed by the Countess who, more dead than alive, sank into a Voltaire armchair. Hermann peeped through a chink. Lizaveta Ivanovna passed close by him, and he heard her hurried steps as she hastened up the little spiral staircase. For a moment his heart was assailed by something like a pricking of conscience, but the emotion was only transitory, and his heart became petrified as before.

The Countess began to undress before her looking-glass. Her rose-bedecked cap was taken off, and then her powdered wig was removed from off her white and closely-cut hair. Hairpins fell in showers around her. Her yellow satin dress, brocaded with silver, fell down at her swollen feet.

Hermann was a witness of the repugnant mysteries of her toilette; at last the Countess was in her night-cap and dressing-gown, and in this costume, more suitable to her age, she appeared less hideous and deformed.

Like all old people in general, the Countess suffered from sleeplessness. Having undressed, she seated herself at the window in a Voltaire armchair and dismissed her maids. The candles were taken away, and once more the room was left with only one lamp burning in it. The Countess sat there looking quite yellow, mumbling with her flaccid lips and swaying to and fro. Her dull eyes expressed complete vacancy of mind, and, looking at her, one would have thought that the rocking of her body was not a voluntary action of her own, but was produced by the action of some concealed galvanic mechanism.

Suddenly the death-like face assumed an inexplicable expression. The lips ceased to tremble, the eyes became animated: before the Countess stood an unknown man.

"Do not be alarmed, for Heaven's sake, do not be alarmed!" said he in a low but distinct voice. "I have no intention of doing you any harm, I have only come to ask a favour of you."

The old woman looked at him in silence, as if she had not heard what he had said. Hermann thought that she was deaf, and bending down towards her ear, he repeated what he had said. The aged Countess remained silent as before.

"You can insure the happiness of my life," continued Hermann, "and it will cost you nothing. I know that you can name three cards in order—"

Hermann stopped. The Countess appeared now to understand what he wanted; she seemed as if seeking for words to reply.

"It was a joke," she replied at last: "I assure you it was only a joke."

"There is no joking about the matter," replied Hermann angrily.

"Remember Chaplitzky, whom you helped to win."

The Countess became visibly uneasy. Her features expressed strong emotion, but they quickly resumed their former immobility.

"Can you not name me these three winning cards?" continued Hermann.

The Countess remained silent; Hermann continued:

"For whom are you preserving your secret? For your grandsons? They are rich enough without it; they do not know the worth of money. Your cards would be of no use to a spendthrift. He who cannot preserve his paternal inheritance, will die in want, even though he had a demon at his service. I am not a man of that sort; I know the value of money. Your three cards will not be thrown away upon me. Come!"...

He paused and tremblingly awaited her reply. The Countess remained silent; Hermann fell upon his knees.

"If your heart has ever known the feeling of love," said he, "if you remember its rapture, if you have ever smiled at the cry of your new-born child, if any human feeling has ever entered into your breast, I entreat you by the feelings of a wife, a lover, a mother, by all that is most sacred in life, not to reject my prayer. Reveal to me your secret. Of what use is it to you?... May be it is connected with some terrible sin with the loss of eternal salvation, with some bargain with the devil... Reflect,—you are old; you have not long to live—I am ready to take your sins upon my soul. Only reveal to me your secret. Remember that the happiness of a man is in your hands, that not only I, but my children, and grandchildren will bless your memory and reverence you as a saint..."

The old Countess answered not a word.

Hermann rose to his feet.

"You old hag!" he exclaimed, grinding his teeth, "then I will make you answer!"

With these words he drew a pistol from his pocket.

At the sight of the pistol, the Countess for the second time exhibited strong emotion. She shook her head and raised her hands as if to protect herself from the shot... then she fell backwards and remained motionless.

"Come, an end to this childish nonsense!" said Hermann, taking hold of her hand. "I ask you for the last time: will you tell me the names of your three cards, or will you not?"

The Countess made no reply. Hermann perceived that she was dead!

IV

Lizaveta Ivanovna was sitting in her room, still in her ball dress, lost in deep thought. On returning home, she had hastily dismissed the chambermaid who very reluctantly came forward to assist her, saying that she would undress herself, and with a trembling heart had gone up to her own room, expecting to find Hermann there, but yet hoping not to find him. At the first glance she convinced herself that he was not there, and she thanked her fate for having prevented him keeping the appointment. She sat down without undressing, and began to recall to mind all the circumstances which in so short a time had carried her so far. It was not three weeks since the time when she first saw the young officer from the window—and yet she was already in correspondence with him, and he had succeeded in inducing her to grant him a nocturnal interview! She knew his name only through his having written it at the bottom of some of his letters; she had never spoken to him, had never heard his voice, and had never heard him spoken of until that evening. But, strange to say, that very evening at the ball, Tomsky, being piqued with the young Princess Pauline N——, who, contrary to her usual custom, did not flirt with him, wished to revenge himself by assuming an air of indifference: he therefore engaged Lizaveta Ivanovna and danced an endless mazurka with her. During the whole of the time he kept teasing her about her partiality for Engineer officers; he assured her that he knew far more than she imagined, and some of his jests were so happily aimed, that Lizaveta thought several times that her secret was known to him.

"From whom have you learnt all this?" she asked, smiling.

"From a friend of a person very well known to you," replied Tomsky, "from a very distinguished man."

"And who is this distinguished man?"

"His name is Hermann."

Lizaveta made no reply; but her hands and feet lost all sense of feeling.

"This Hermann," continued Tomsky, "is a man of romantic personality. He has the profile of a Napoleon, and the soul of a Mephistopheles. I believe that he has at least three crimes upon his conscience... How pale you have become!"

"I have a headache... But what did this Hermann—or whatever his name is—tell you?"

"Hermann is very much dissatisfied with his friend: he says that in his place he would act very differently... I even think that Hermann himself has designs upon you; at least, he listens very attentively to all that his friend has to say about you."

"And where has he seen me?"

"In church, perhaps; or on the parade—God alone knows where. It may have been in your room, while you were asleep, for there is nothing that he—"

Three ladies approaching him with the question: "oubli ou regret?" interrupted the conversation, which had become so tantalisingly interesting to Lizaveta.

The lady chosen by Tomsky was the Princess Pauline herself. She succeeded in effecting a reconciliation with him during the numerous turns of the dance, after which he conducted her to her chair. On returning to his place, Tomsky thought no more either of Hermann or Lizaveta. She longed to renew the interrupted conversation, but the mazurka came to an end, and shortly afterwards the old Countess took her departure.

Tomsky's words were nothing more than the customary small talk of the dance, but they sank deep into the soul of the young dreamer. The portrait, sketched by Tomsky, coincided with the picture she had formed within her own mind, and thanks to the latest romances, the ordinary countenance of her admirer became invested with attributes capable of alarming her and fascinating her imagination at the same time. She was now sitting with her bare arms crossed and with her head, still adorned with flowers, sunk upon her uncovered bosom. Suddenly the door opened and Hermann entered. She shuddered.

"Where were you?" she asked in a terrified whisper.

"In the old Countess's bedroom," replied Hermann: "I have just left her. The Countess is dead."

"My God! What do you say?"

"And I am afraid," added Hermann, "that I am the cause of her death."

Lizaveta looked at him, and Tomsky's words found an echo in her soul: "This man has at least three crimes upon his conscience!" Hermann sat down by the window near her, and related all that had happened.

Lizaveta listened to him in terror. So all those passionate letters, those ardent desires, this bold obstinate pursuit—all this was not love! Money—that was what his soul yearned for! She could not satisfy his desire and make him happy! The poor girl had been nothing but the blind tool of a robber, of the murderer of her aged benefactress!... She wept bitter tears of agonised repentance. Hermann gazed at her in silence: his heart, too, was a prey to violent emotion, but neither the tears of the poor girl, nor the wonderful charm of her beauty, enhanced by her grief, could produce any impression upon his hardened soul. He felt no pricking of conscience at the thought of the dead old woman. One thing only grieved him: the irreparable loss of the secret from which he had expected to obtain great wealth.

"You are a monster!" said Lizaveta at last.

"I did not wish for her death," replied Hermann: "my pistol was not loaded."

Both remained silent.

The day began to dawn. Lizaveta extinguished her candle: a pale light illumined her room. She wiped her tear-stained eyes and raised them towards Hermann: he was sitting near the window, with his arms crossed and with a fierce frown upon his forehead. In this attitude he bore a striking resemblance to the portrait of Napoleon. This resemblance struck Lizaveta even.

"How shall I get you out of the house?" said she at last. "I thought of conducting you down the secret staircase, but in that case it would be necessary to go through the Countess's bedroom, and I am afraid."

"Tell me how to find this secret staircase—I will go alone."

Lizaveta arose, took from her drawer a key, handed it to Hermann and gave him the necessary instructions. Hermann pressed her cold, limp hand, kissed her bowed head, and left the room.

He descended the winding staircase, and once more entered the Countess's bedroom. The dead old lady sat as if petrified; her face expressed profound tranquillity. Hermann stopped before her, and gazed long and earnestly at her, as if he wished to convince himself of the terrible reality; at last he entered the cabinet, felt behind the tapestry for the door, and then began to descend the dark staircase, filled with strange emotions. "Down this very staircase," thought he, "perhaps coming from the very same room, and at this very same hour sixty years ago, there may have glided, in an embroidered coat, with his hair dressed à l'oiseau royal and pressing to his heart his three-cornered hat, some young gallant, who has long been mouldering in the grave, but the heart of his aged mistress has only to-day ceased to beat..."

At the bottom of the staircase Hermann found a door, which he opened with a key, and then traversed a corridor which conducted him into the street.

V

Three days after the fatal night, at nine o'clock in the morning, Hermann repaired to the Convent of ——, where the last honours were to be paid to the mortal remains of the old Countess. Although feeling no remorse, he could not altogether stifle the voice of conscience, which said to him: "You are the murderer of the old woman!" In spite of his entertaining very little religious belief, he was exceedingly superstitious; and believing that the dead Countess might exercise an evil influence on his life, he resolved to be present at her obsequies in order to implore her pardon.

The church was full. It was with difficulty that Hermann made his way through the crowd of people. The coffin was placed upon a rich catafalque beneath a velvet baldachin. The deceased Countess lay within it, with her hands crossed upon her breast, with a lace cap upon her head and dressed in a white satin robe. Around the catafalque stood the members of her household: the servants in black caftans, with armorial ribbons upon their shoulders, and candles in their hands; the relatives—children, grandchildren, and great-grandchildren—in deep mourning.

Nobody wept; tears would have been une affectation. The Countess was so old, that her death could have surprised nobody, and her relatives had long looked upon her as being out of the world. A famous preacher pronounced the funeral sermon. In simple and touching words he described the peaceful passing away of the righteous, who had passed long years in calm preparation for a Christian end. "The angel of death found her," said the orator, "engaged in pious meditation and waiting for the midnight bridegroom."

The service concluded amidst profound silence. The relatives went forward first to take farewell of the corpse. Then followed the numerous guests, who had come to render the last homage to her who for so many years had been a participator in their frivolous amusements. After these followed the members of the Countess's household. The last of these was an old woman of the same age as the deceased. Two young women led her forward by the hand. She had not strength enough to bow down to the ground—she merely shed a few tears and kissed the cold hand of her mistress.

Hermann now resolved to approach the coffin. He knelt down upon the cold stones and remained in that position for some minutes; at last he arose, as pale as the deceased Countess herself; he ascended the steps of the catafalque and bent over the corpse... At that moment it seemed to him that the dead woman darted a mocking look at him and winked with one eye. Hermann started back, took a false step and fell to the ground. Several persons hurried forward and raised him up. At the same moment Lizaveta Ivanovna was borne fainting into the porch of the church. This episode disturbed for some minutes the solemnity of the gloomy ceremony. Among the congregation arose a deep murmur, and a tall thin chamberlain, a near relative of the deceased, whispered in the ear of an Englishman who was standing near him, that the young officer was a natural son of the Countess, to which the Englishman coldly replied: "Oh!"

During the whole of that day, Hermann was strangely excited. Repairing to an out-of-the-way restaurant to dine, he drank a great deal of wine, contrary to his usual custom, in the hope of deadening his inward agitation. But the wine only served to excite his imagination still more. On returning home, he threw himself upon his bed without undressing, and fell into a deep sleep.

When he woke up it was already night, and the moon was shining into the room. He looked at his watch: it was a quarter to three. Sleep had left him; he sat down upon his bed and thought of the funeral of the old Countess.

At that moment somebody in the street looked in at his window, and immediately passed on again. Hermann paid no attention to this incident. A few moments afterwards he heard the door of his ante-room open. Hermann thought that it was his orderly, drunk as usual, returning from some nocturnal expedition, but presently he heard footsteps that were unknown to him: somebody was walking softly over the floor in slippers. The door opened, and a woman dressed in white, entered the room. Hermann mistook her for his old nurse, and wondered what could bring her there at that hour of the night. But the white woman glided rapidly across the room and stood before him—and Hermann recognised the Countess!

"I have come to you against my wish," she said in a firm voice: "but I have been ordered to grant your request. Three, seven, ace, will win for you if played in succession, but only on these conditions: that you do not play more than one card in twenty-four hours, and that you never play again during the rest of your life. I forgive you my death, on condition that you marry my companion, Lizaveta Ivanovna."

With these words she turned round very quietly, walked with a shuffling gait towards the door and disappeared. Hermann heard the street-door open and shut, and again he saw some one look in at him through the window.

For a long time Hermann could not recover himself. He then rose up and entered the next room. His orderly was lying asleep upon the floor, and he had much difficulty in waking him. The orderly was drunk as usual, and no information could be obtained from him. The street-door was locked. Hermann returned to his room, lit his candle, and wrote down all the details of his vision.

VI

Two fixed ideas can no more exist together in the moral world than two bodies can occupy one and the same place in the physical world. "Three, seven, ace," soon drove out of Hermann's mind the thought of the dead Countess. "Three, seven, ace," were perpetually running through his head and continually being repeated by his lips. If he saw a young girl, he would say: "How slender she is! quite like the three of hearts." If anybody asked: "What is the time?" he would reply: "Five minutes to seven." Every stout man that he saw reminded him of the ace. "Three, seven, ace" haunted him in his sleep, and assumed all possible shapes. The threes bloomed before him in the forms of magnificent flowers, the sevens were represented by Gothic portals, and the aces became transformed into gigantic spiders. One thought alone occupied his whole mind—to make a profitable use of the secret which he had purchased so dearly. He thought of applying for a furlough so as to travel abroad. He wanted to go to Paris and tempt fortune in some of the public gambling-houses that abounded there. Chance spared him all this trouble.

There was in Moscow a society of rich gamesters, presided over by the celebrated Chekalinsky, who had passed all his life at the card-table and had amassed millions, accepting bills of exchange for his winnings and paying his losses in ready money. His long experience secured for him the confidence of his companions, and his open house, his famous cook, and his agreeable and fascinating manners gained for him the respect of the public. He came to St. Petersburg. The young men of the capital flocked to his rooms, forgetting balls for cards, and preferring the emotions of faro to the seductions of flirting. Narumov conducted Hermann to Chekalinsky's residence.

They passed through a suite of magnificent rooms, filled with attentive domestics. The place was crowded. Generals and Privy Counsellors were playing at whist; young men were lolling carelessly upon the velvet-covered sofas, eating ices and smoking pipes. In the drawing-room, at the head of a long table, around which were assembled about a score of players, sat the master of the house keeping the bank. He was a man of about sixty years of age, of a very dignified appearance; his head was covered with silvery-white hair; his full, florid countenance expressed good-nature, and his eyes twinkled with a perpetual smile. Narumov introduced Hermann to him. Chekalinsky shook him by the hand in a friendly manner, requested him not to stand on ceremony, and then went on dealing.

The game occupied some time. On the table lay more than thirty cards. Chekalinsky paused after each throw, in order to give the players time to arrange their cards and note down their losses, listened politely to their requests, and more politely still, put straight the corners of cards that some player's hand had chanced to bend. At last the game was finished. Chekalinsky shuffled the cards and prepared to deal again.

"Will you allow me to take a card?" said Hermann, stretching out his hand from behind a stout gentleman who was punting.

Chekalinsky smiled and bowed silently, as a sign of acquiescence. Narumov laughingly congratulated Hermann on his abjuration of that abstention from cards which he had practised for so long a period, and wished him a lucky beginning.

"Stake!" said Hermann, writing some figures with chalk on the back of his card.

"How much?" asked the banker, contracting the muscles of his eyes; "excuse me, I cannot see quite clearly."

"Forty-seven thousand rubles," replied Hermann.

At these words every head in the room turned suddenly round, and all eyes were fixed upon Hermann.

"He has taken leave of his senses!" thought Narumov.

"Allow me to inform you," said Chekalinsky, with his eternal smile, "that you are playing very high; nobody here has ever staked more than two hundred and seventy-five rubles at once."

"Very well," replied Hermann; "but do you accept my card or not?"

Chekalinsky bowed in token of consent.

"I only wish to observe," said he, "that although I have the greatest confidence in my friends, I can only play against ready money. For my own part, I am quite convinced that your word is sufficient, but for the sake of the order of the game, and to facilitate the reckoning up, I must ask you to put the money on your card."

Hermann drew from his pocket a banknote and handed it to Chekalinsky, who, after examining it in a cursory manner, placed it on Hermann's card.

He began to deal. On the right a nine turned up, and on the left a three.

"I have won!" said Hermann, showing his card.

A murmur of astonishment arose among the players. Chekalinsky frowned, but the smile quickly returned to his face.

"Do you wish me to settle with you?" he said to Hermann.

"If you please," replied the latter.

Chekalinsky drew from his pocket a number of banknotes and paid at once. Hermann took up his money and left the table. Narumov could not recover from his astonishment. Hermann drank a glass of lemonade and returned home.

The next evening he again repaired to Chekalinsky's. The host was dealing. Hermann walked up to the table; the punters immediately made room for him. Chekalinsky greeted him with a gracious bow.

Hermann waited for the next deal, took a card and placed upon it his forty-seven thousand roubles, together with his winnings of the previous evening.

Chekalinsky began to deal. A knave turned up on the right, a seven on the left.

Hermann showed his seven.

There was a general exclamation. Chekalinsky was evidently ill at ease, but he counted out the ninety-four thousand rubles and handed them over to Hermann, who pocketed them in the coolest manner possible and immediately left the house.

The next evening Hermann appeared again at the table. Every one was expecting him. The generals and Privy Counsellors left their whist in order to watch such extraordinary play. The young officers quitted their sofas, and even the servants crowded into the room. All pressed round Hermann. The other players left off punting, impatient to see how it would end. Hermann stood at the table and prepared to play alone against the pale, but still smiling Chekalinsky. Each opened a pack of cards. Chekalinsky shuffled. Hermann took a card and covered it with a pile of banknotes. It was like a duel. Deep silence reigned around.

Chekalinsky began to deal; his hands trembled. On the right a queen turned up, and on the left an ace.

"Ace has won!" cried Hermann, showing his card.

"Your queen has lost," said Chekalinsky, politely.

Hermann started; instead of an ace, there lay before him the queen of spades! He could not believe his eyes, nor could he understand how he had made such a mistake.

At that moment it seemed to him that the queen of spades smiled ironically and winked her eye at him. He was struck by her remarkable resemblance...

"The old Countess!" he exclaimed, seized with terror.

Chekalinsky gathered up his winnings. For some time, Hermann remained perfectly motionless. When at last he left the table, there was a general commotion in the room.

"Splendidly punted!" said the players. Chekalinsky shuffled the cards afresh, and the game went on as usual.

* * * * *

Hermann went out of his mind, and is now confined in room Number 17 of the Obukhov Hospital. He never answers any questions, but he constantly mutters with unusual rapidity: "Three, seven, ace!" "Three, seven, queen!"

Lizaveta Ivanovna has married a very amiable young man, a son of the former steward of the old Countess. He is in the service of the State somewhere, and is in receipt of a good income. Lizaveta is also supporting a poor relative.

Tomsky has been promoted to the rank of captain, and has become the husband of the Princess Pauline.

THE CLOAK

BY NIKOLAY V. GOGOL

In the department of——, but it is better not to mention the department. The touchiest things in the world are departments, regiments, courts of justice, in a word, all branches of public service. Each individual nowadays thinks all society insulted in his person. Quite recently, a complaint was received from a district chief of police in which he plainly demonstrated that all the imperial institutions were going to the dogs, and that the Czar's sacred name was being taken in vain; and in proof he appended to the complaint a romance, in which the district chief of police is made to appear about once in every ten pages, and sometimes in a downright drunken condition. Therefore, in order to avoid all unpleasantness, it will be better to designate the department in question, as a certain department.

So, in a certain department there was a certain official—not a very notable one, it must be allowed—short of stature, somewhat pock-marked, red-haired, and mole-eyed, with a bald forehead, wrinkled cheeks, and a complexion of the kind known as sanguine. The St. Petersburg climate was responsible for this. As for his official rank—with us Russians the rank comes first—he was what is called a perpetual titular councillor, over which, as is well known, some writers make merry and crack their jokes, obeying the praiseworthy custom of attacking those who cannot bite back.

His family name was Bashmachkin. This name is evidently derived from bashmak (shoe); but, when, at what time, and in what manner, is not known. His father and grandfather, and all the Bashmachkins, always wore boots, which were resoled two or three times a year. His name was Akaky Akakiyevich. It may strike the reader as rather singular and far-fetched; but he may rest assured that it was by no means far-fetched, and that the circumstances were such that it would have been impossible to give him any other.

This was how it came about.

Akaky Akakiyevich was born, if my memory fails me not, in the evening on the 23rd of March. His mother, the wife of a Government official, and a very fine woman, made all due arrangements for having the child baptised. She was lying on the bed opposite the door; on her right stood the godfather, Ivan Ivanovich Eroshkin, a most estimable man, who served as the head clerk of the senate; and the godmother, Arina Semyonovna Bielobrinshkova, the wife of an officer of the quarter, and a woman of rare virtues. They offered the mother her choice of three names, Mokiya, Sossiya, or that the child should be called after the martyr Khozdazat. "No," said the good woman, "all those names are poor." In order to please her, they opened the calendar at another place; three more names appeared, Triphily, Dula, and Varakhasy. "This is awful," said the old woman. "What names! I truly never heard the like. I might have put up with Varadat or Varukh, but not Triphily and Varakhasy!" They turned to another page and found Pavsikakhy and Vakhtisy. "Now I see," said the old woman, "that it is plainly fate. And since such is the case, it will be better to name him after his father. His father's name was Akaky, so let his son's name be Akaky too." In this manner he became Akaky Akakiyevich. They christened the child, whereat he wept, and made a grimace, as though he foresaw that he was to be a titular councillor.

In this manner did it all come about. We have mentioned it in order that the reader might see for himself that it was a case of necessity, and that it was utterly impossible to give him any other name.

When and how he entered the department, and who appointed him, no one could remember. However much the directors and chiefs of all kinds were changed, he was always to be seen in the same place, the same attitude, the same occupation—always the letter-copying clerk—so that it was afterwards affirmed that he had been born in uniform with a bald head. No respect was shown him in the department. The porter not only did not rise from his seat when he passed, but never even glanced at him, any more than if a fly had flown through the reception-room. His superiors treated him in coolly despotic fashion. Some insignificant assistant to the head clerk would thrust a paper under his nose without so much as saying, "Copy," or, "Here's an interesting little case," or anything else agreeable, as is customary amongst well-bred officials. And he took it, looking only at the paper, and not observing who handed it to him, or whether he had the right to do so; simply took it, and set about copying it.

The young officials laughed at and made fun of him, so far as their official wit permitted; told in his presence various stories concocted about him, and about his landlady, an old woman of seventy; declared that she beat him; asked when the wedding was to be; and strewed bits of paper over his head, calling them snow. But Akaky Akakiyevich answered not a word, any more than if there had been no one there besides himself. It even had no effect upon his work. Amid all these annoyances he never made a single mistake in a letter. But if the joking became wholly unbearable, as when they jogged his head, and prevented his attending to his work, he would exclaim:

"Leave me alone! Why do you insult me?"

And there was something strange in the words and the voice in which they were uttered. There was in it something which moved to pity; so much so that one young man, a newcomer, who, taking pattern by the others, had permitted himself to make sport of Akaky, suddenly stopped short, as though all about him had undergone a transformation, and presented itself in a different aspect. Some unseen force repelled him from the comrades whose acquaintance he had made, on the supposition that they were decent, well-bred men. Long afterwards, in his gayest moments, there recurred to his mind the little official with the bald forehead, with his heart-rending words, "Leave me alone! Why do you insult me?" In these moving words, other words resounded—"I am thy brother." And the young man covered his face with his hand; and many a time afterwards, in the course of his life, shuddered at seeing how much inhumanity there is in man, how much savage coarseness is concealed beneath refined, cultured, worldly refinement, and even, O God! in that man whom the world acknowledges as honourable and upright.

It would be difficult to find another man who lived so entirely for his duties. It is not enough to say that Akaky laboured with zeal; no, he laboured with love. In his copying, he found a varied and agreeable employment. Enjoyment was written on his face; some letters were even favourites with him; and when he encountered these, he smiled, winked, and worked with his lips, till it seemed as though each letter might be read in his face, as his pen traced it. If his pay had been in proportion to his zeal, he would, perhaps, to his great surprise, have been made even a councillor of state. But he worked, as his companions, the wits, put it, like a horse in a mill.

However, it would be untrue to say that no attention was paid to him. One director being a kindly man, and desirous of rewarding him for his long service, ordered him to be given something more important than mere copying. So he was ordered to make a report of an already concluded affair, to another department; the duty consisting simply in changing the heading and altering a few words from the first to the third person. This caused him so much toil, that he broke into a perspiration, rubbed his forehead, and finally said, "No, give me rather something to copy." After that they let him copy on forever.

Outside this copying, it appeared that nothing existed for him. He gave no thought to his clothes. His uniform was not green, but a sort of rusty-meal colour. The collar was low, so that his neck, in spite of the fact that it was not long, seemed inordinately so as it emerged from it, like the necks of the plaster cats which pedlars carry about on their heads. And something was always sticking to his uniform, either a bit of hay or some trifle. Moreover, he had a peculiar knack, as he walked along the street, of arriving beneath a window just as all sorts of rubbish was being flung out of it; hence he always bore about on his hat scraps of melon rinds, and other such articles. Never once in his life did he give heed to what was going on every day to the street; while it is well known that his young brother officials trained the range of their glances till they could see when any one's trouser-straps came undone upon the opposite sidewalk, which always brought a malicious smile to their faces. But Akaky Akakiyevich saw in all things the clean, even strokes of his written lines; and only when a horse thrust his nose, from some unknown quarter, over his shoulder, and sent a whole gust of wind down his neck from his nostrils, did he observe that he was not in the middle of a line, but in the middle of the street.

On reaching home, he sat down at once at the table, sipped his cabbage-soup up quickly, and swallowed a bit of beef with onions, never noticing their taste, and gulping down everything with flies and anything else which the Lord happened to send at the moment. When he saw that his stomach was beginning to swell, he rose from the table, and copied papers which he had brought home. If there happened to be none, he took copies for himself, for his own gratification, especially if the document was noteworthy, not on account of its style, but of its being addressed to some distinguished person.

Even at the hour when the grey St. Petersburg sky had quite disappeared, and all the official world had eaten or dined, each as he could, in accordance with the salary he received and his own fancy; when, all were resting from the department jar of pens, running to and fro, for their own and other people's indispensable occupations', and from all the work that an uneasy man makes willingly for himself, rather than what is necessary; when, officials hasten to dedicate to pleasure the time which is left to them, one bolder than the rest, going to the theatre; another; into the street looking under the bonnets; another, wasting his evening in compliments to some pretty girl, the star of a small official circle; another—and this is the common case of all—

visiting his comrades on the third or fourth floor, in two small rooms with an ante-room or kitchen, and some pretensions to fashion, such as a lamp or some other trifle which has cost many a sacrifice of dinner or pleasure trip; in a word, at the hour when all officials disperse among the contracted quarters of their friends, to play whist, as they sip their tea from glasses with a kopek's worth of sugar, smoke long pipes, relate at time some bits of gossip which a Russian man can never, under any circumstances, refrain from, and when there is nothing else to talk of, repeat eternal anecdotes about the commandant to whom they had sent word that the tails of the horses on the Falconet Monument had been cut off; when all strive to divert themselves, Akaky Akakiyevich indulged in no kind of diversion. No one could even say that he had seen him at any kind of evening party. Having written to his heart's content, he lay down to sleep, smiling at the thought of the coming day—of what God might send him to copy on the morrow.

Thus flowed on the peaceful life of the man, who, with a salary of four hundred rubles, understood how to be content with his lot; and thus it would have continued to flow on, perhaps, to extreme old age, were it not that there are various ills strewn along the path of life for titular councillors as well as for private, actual, court, and every other species of councillor, even to those who never give any advice or take any themselves.

There exists in St. Petersburg a powerful foe of all who receive a salary of four hundred rubles a year, or there-abouts. This foe is no other than the Northern cold, although it is said to be very healthy. At nine o'clock in the morning, at the very hour when the streets are filled with men bound for the various official departments, it begins to bestow such powerful and piercing nips on all noses impartially, that the poor officials really do not know what to do with them. At an hour, when the foreheads of even those who occupy exalted positions ache with the cold, and tears start to their eyes, the poor titular councillors are sometimes quite unprotected. Their only salvation lies in traversing as quickly as possible, in their thin little cloaks, five or six streets, and then warming their feet in the porter's room, and so thawing all their talents and qualifications for official service, which had become frozen on the way.

Akaky Akakiyevich had felt for some time

that his back and shoulders were paining with peculiar poignancy, in spite of the fact that he tried to traverse the distance with all possible speed. He began finally to wonder whether the fault did not lie in his cloak. He examined it thoroughly at home, and discovered that in two places, namely, on the back and shoulders, it had become thin as gauze. The cloth was worn to such a degree that he could see through it, and the lining had fallen into pieces. You must know that Akaky Akakiyevich's cloak served as an object of ridicule to the officials. They even refused it the noble name of cloak, and called it a cape. In fact, it was of singular make, its collar diminishing year by year to serve to patch its other parts. The patching did not exhibit great skill on the part of the tailor, and was, in fact, baggy and ugly. Seeing how the matter stood, Akaky Akakiyevich decided that it would be necessary to take the cloak to Petrovich, the tailor, who lived somewhere on the fourth floor up a dark staircase, and who, in spite of his having but one eye and pock-marks all over his face, busied himself with considerable success in repairing the trousers and coats of officials and others; that is to say, when he was sober and not nursing some other scheme in his head.

It is not necessary to say much about this tailor, but as it is the custom to have the character of each personage in a novel clearly defined there is no help for it, so here is Petrovich the tailor. At first he was called only Grigory, and was some gentleman's serf. He commenced calling himself Petrovich from the time when he received his free papers, and further began to drink heavily on all holidays, at first on the great ones, and then on all church festivals without discrimination, wherever a cross stood in the calendar. On this point he was faithful to ancestral custom; and when quarrelling with his wife, he called her a low female and a German. As we have mentioned his wife, it will be necessary to say a word or two about her. Unfortunately, little is known of her beyond the fact that Petrovich had a wife, who wore a cap and a dress, but could not lay claim to beauty, at least, no one but the soldiers of the guard even looked under her cap when they met her.

Ascending the staircase which led to Petrovich's room—which staircase was all soaked with dish-water and reeked with the smell of spirits which affects the eyes, and is an inevitable adjunct to all dark stairways in St. Petersburg houses—ascending the stairs, Akaky Akakiyevich pondered how much Petrovich would ask, and mentally resolved not to give more than two rubles. The door was open, for the mistress, in cooking some fish, had raised such a smoke in the kitchen that not even the beetles were visible. Akaky Akakiyevich passed through the kitchen unperceived, even by the housewife, and at length reached a room where he beheld Petrovich seated on a large unpainted table, with his legs tucked under him like a Turkish pasha. His feet were bare, after the fashion of tailors as they sit at work; and the first thing which caught the eye was his thumb, with a deformed nail thick and strong as a turtle's shell. About Petrovich's neck hung a skein of silk and thread, and upon his knees lay some old garment. He had been trying unsuccessfully for three minutes to thread his needle, and was enraged at the darkness and even at the thread, growling in a low voice, "It won't go through, the barbarian! you pricked me, you rascal!"

Akaky Akakiyevich was vexed at arriving at the precise moment when Petrovich was angry. He liked to order something of Petrovich when he was a little downhearted, or, as his wife expressed it, "when he had settled himself with brandy, the one-eyed devil!" Under such circumstances Petrovich generally came down in his price very readily, and even bowed and returned thanks. Afterwards, to be sure, his wife would come, complaining that her husband had been drunk, and so had fixed the price too low; but, if only a ten-kopek piece were added then the matter would be settled. But now it appeared that Petrovich was in a sober condition, and therefore rough, taciturn, and inclined to demand, Satan only knows what price. Akaky Akakiyevich felt this, and would gladly have beat a retreat, but he was in for it. Petrovich screwed up his one eye very intently at him, and Akaky Akakiyevich involuntarily said, "How do you do, Petrovich?"

"I wish you a good morning, sir," said Petrovich squinting at Akaky

Akakiyevich's hands, to see what sort of booty he had brought.

"Ah! I—to you, Petrovich, this—" It must be known that Akaky Akakiyevich expressed himself chiefly by prepositions, adverbs, and scraps of phrases which had no meaning whatever. If the matter was a very difficult one, he had a habit of never completing his sentences, so that frequently, having begun a phrase with the words, "This, in fact, is quite—" he forgot to go on, thinking he had already finished it.

"What is it?" asked Petrovich, and with his one eye scanned Akaky Akakiyevich's whole uniform from the collar down to the cuffs, the back, the tails and the button-holes, all of which were well known to him, since they were his own handiwork. Such is the habit of tailors; it is the first thing they do on meeting one.

"But I, here, this—Petrovich—a cloak, cloth—here you see, everywhere, in different places, it is quite strong—it is a little dusty and looks old, but it is new, only here in one place it is a little—on the back, and here on one of the shoulders, it is a little worn, yes, here on this shoulder it is a little—do you see? That is all. And a little work—"

Petrovich took the cloak, spread it out, to begin with, on the table, looked at it hard, shook his head, reached out his hand to the window-sill for his snuff-box, adorned with the portrait of some general, though what general is unknown, for the place where the face should have been had been rubbed through by the finger and a square bit of paper had been pasted over it. Having taken a pinch of snuff, Petrovich held up the cloak, and inspected it against the light, and again shook his head. Then he turned it, lining upwards, and shook his head once more. After which he again lifted the general-adorned lid with its bit of pasted paper, and having stuffed his nose with snuff, dosed and put away the snuff-box, and said finally, "No, it is impossible to mend it. It is a wretched garment!"

Akaky Akakiyevich's heart sank at these words.

"Why is it impossible, Petrovich?" he said, almost in the pleading voice of a child. "All that ails it is, that it is worn on the shoulders. You must have some pieces—"

"Yes, patches could be found, patches are easily found," said Petrovich, "but there's nothing to sew them to. The thing is completely rotten. If you put a needle to it—see, it will give way."

"Let it give way, and you can put on another patch at once."

"But there is nothing to put the patches on to. There's no use in strengthening it. It is too far gone. It's lucky that it's cloth, for, if the wind were to blow, it would fly away."

"Well, strengthen it again. How this, in fact—"

"No," said Petrovich decisively, "there is nothing to be done with it. It's a thoroughly bad job. You'd better, when the cold winter weather comes on, make yourself some gaiters out of it, because stockings are not warm. The Germans invented them in order to make more money." Petrovich loved on all occasions to have a fling at the Germans. "But it is plain you must have a new cloak."

At the word "new" all grew dark before Akaky Akakiyevich's eyes, and everything in the room began to whirl round. The only thing he saw clearly was the general with the paper face on the lid of Petrovich's snuff-box. "A new one?" said he, as if still in a dream. "Why, I have no money for that."

"Yes, a new one," said Petrovich, with barbarous composure.

"Well, if it came to a new one, how—it—"

"You mean how much would it cost?"

"Yes."

"Well, you would have to lay out a hundred and fifty or more," said Petrovich, and pursed up his lips significantly. He liked to produce powerful effects, liked to stun utterly and suddenly, and then to glance sideways to see what face the stunned person would put on the matter.

"A hundred and fifty rubles for a cloak!" shrieked poor Akaky Akakiyevich, perhaps for the first time in his life, for his voice had always been distinguished for softness.

"Yes, sir," said Petrovich, "for any kind of cloak. If you have a marten fur on the collar, or a silk-lined hood, it will mount up to two hundred."

"Petrovich, please," said Akaky Akakiyevich in a beseeching tone, not hearing, and not trying to hear, Petrovich's words, and disregarding all his "effects," "some repairs, in order that it may wear yet a little longer."

"No, it would only be a waste of time and money," said Petrovich. And Akaky Akakiyevich went away after these words, utterly discouraged. But Petrovich stood for some time after his departure, with significantly compressed lips, and without betaking himself to his work, satisfied that he would not be dropped, and an artistic tailor employed.

Akaky Akakiyevich went out into the street as if in a dream. "Such an affair!" he said to himself. "I did not think it had come to—" and then after a pause, he added, "Well, so it is! see what it has come to at last! and I never imagined that it was so!" Then followed a long silence, after which he exclaimed, "Well, so it is! see what already—nothing unexpected that—it would be nothing—what a strange circumstance!" So saying, instead of going home, he went in exactly the opposite direction without suspecting it. On the way, a chimney-sweep bumped up against him, and blackened his shoulder, and a whole hatful of rubbish landed on him from the top of a house which was building. He did not notice it, and only when he ran against a watchman, who, having planted his halberd beside him, was shaking some snuff from his box into his horny hand, did he recover himself a little, and that because the watchman said, "Why are you poking yourself into a man's very face? Haven't you the pavement?" This caused him to look about him, and turn towards home.

There only, he finally began to collect his thoughts, and to survey his position in its clear and actual light, and to argue with himself, sensibly and frankly, as with a reasonable friend, with whom one can discuss private and personal matters. "No," said Akaky Akakiyevich, "it is impossible to reason with Petrovich now. He is that—evidently, his wife has been beating him. I'd better go to him on Sunday morning. After Saturday night he will be a little cross-eyed and sleepy, for he will want to get drunk, and his wife won't give him any money, and at such a time, a ten-kopek piece in his hand will—he will become more fit to reason with, and then the cloak and that—" Thus argued Akaky Akakiyevich with himself regained his courage, and waited until the first Sunday, when, seeing from afar that Petrovich's wife had left the house, he went straight to him.

Petrovich's eye was indeed very much askew after Saturday. His head drooped, and he was very sleepy; but for all that, as soon as he knew what it was a question of, it seemed as though Satan jogged his memory. "Impossible," said he. "Please to order a new one." Thereupon Akaky Akakiyevich handed over the ten-kopek piece. "Thank you, sir. I will drink your good health," said Petrovich. "But as for the cloak, don't trouble yourself about it; it is good for nothing. I will make you a capital new one, so let us settle about it now."

Akaky Akakiyevich was still for mending it, but Petrovich would not hear of it, and said, "I shall certainly have to make you a new one, and you may depend upon it that I shall do my best. It may even be, as the fashion goes, that the collar can be fastened by silver hooks under a flap."

Then Akaky Akakiyevich saw that it was impossible to get along without a new cloak, and his spirit sank utterly. How, in fact, was it to be done? Where was the money to come from? He must have some new trousers, and pay a debt of long standing to the shoemaker for putting new tops to his old boots, and he must order three shirts from the seamstress, and a couple of pieces of linen. In short, all his money must be spent. And even if the director should be so kind as to order him to receive forty-five or even fifty rubles instead of forty, it would be a mere nothing, a mere drop in the ocean towards the funds necessary for a cloak, although he knew that Petrovich was often wrong-headed enough to blurt out some outrageous price, so that even his own wife could not refrain from exclaiming, “Have you lost your senses, you fool?” At one time he would not work at any price, and now it was quite likely that he had named a higher sum than the cloak would cost.

But although he knew that Petrovich would undertake to make a cloak for eighty rubles, still, where was he to get the eighty rubles from? He might possibly manage half. Yes, half might be procured, but where was the other half to come from? But the reader must first be told where the first half came from.

Akaky Akakiyevich had a habit of putting, for every ruble he spent, a groschen into a small box, fastened with lock and key, and with a slit in the top for the reception of money. At the end of every half-year he counted over the heap of coppers, and changed it for silver. This he had done for a long time, and in the course of years, the sum had mounted up to over forty rubles. Thus he had one half on hand. But where was he to find the other half? Where was he to get another forty rubles from? Akaky Akakiyevich thought and thought, and decided that it would be necessary to curtail his ordinary expenses, for the space of one year at least, to dispense with tea in the evening, to burn no candles, and, if there was anything which he must do, to go into his landlady's room, and work by her light. When he went into the street, he must walk as lightly as he could, and as cautiously, upon the stones, almost upon tiptoe, in order not to wear his heels down in too short a time. He must give the laundress as little to wash as possible; and, in order not to wear out his clothes, he must take them off as soon as he got home, and wear only his cotton dressing-gown, which had been long and carefully saved.

To tell the truth, it was a little hard for him at first to accustom himself to these deprivations. But he got used to them at length, after a fashion, and all went smoothly. He even got used to being hungry in the evening, but he made up for it by treating himself, so to say, in spirit, by bearing ever in mind the idea of his future cloak. From that time forth, his existence seemed to become, in some way, fuller, as if he were married, or as if some other man lived in him, as if, in fact, he were not alone, and some pleasant friend had consented to travel along life's path with him, the friend being no other than the cloak, with thick wadding and a strong lining incapable of wearing out. He became more lively, and even his character grew firmer, like that of a man who has made up his mind, and set himself a goal. From his face and gait, doubt and indecision, all hesitating and wavering disappeared of themselves. Fire gleamed in his eyes, and occasionally the boldest and most daring ideas flitted through his mind. Why not, for instance, have marten fur on the collar? The thought of this almost made him absent-minded. Once, in copying a letter, he nearly made a mistake, so that he exclaimed almost aloud, "Ugh!" and crossed himself. Once, in the course of every month, he had a conference with Petrovich on the subject of the cloak, where it would be better to buy the cloth, and the colour, and the price. He always returned home satisfied, though troubled, reflecting that the time would come at last when it could all be bought, and then the cloak made.

The affair progressed more briskly than he had expected. For beyond all his hopes, the director awarded neither forty nor forty-five rubles for Akaky Akakiyevich's share, but sixty. Whether he suspected that Akaky Akakiyevich needed a cloak, or whether it was merely chance, at all events, twenty extra rubles were by this means provided. This circumstance hastened matters. Two or three months more of hunger and Akaky Akakiyevich had accumulated about eighty rubles. His heart, generally so quiet, began to throb. On the first possible day, he went shopping in company with Petrovich. They bought some very good cloth, and at a reasonable rate too, for they had been considering the matter for six months, and rarely let a month pass without their visiting the shops to enquire prices. Petrovich himself said that no better cloth could be had. For lining, they selected a cotton stuff, but so firm and thick, that Petrovich declared it to be better than silk, and even prettier and more glossy. They did not buy the marten fur, because it was, in fact, dear, but in its stead, they picked out the very best of cat-skin which could be found in the shop, and which might, indeed, be taken for marten at a distance.

Petrovich worked at the cloak two whole weeks, for there was a great deal of quilting; otherwise it would have been finished sooner. He charged twelve rubles for the job, it could not possibly have been done for less. It was all sewed with silk, in small, double seams, and Petrovich went over each seam afterwards with his own teeth, stamping in various patterns.

It was—it is difficult to say precisely on what day, but probably the most glorious one in Akaky Akakiyevich's life, when Petrovich at length brought home the cloak. He brought it in the morning, before the hour when it was necessary to start for the department. Never did a cloak arrive so exactly in the nick of time, for the severe cold had set in, and it seemed to threaten to increase. Petrovich brought the cloak himself as befits a good tailor. On his countenance was a significant expression, such as Akaky Akakiyevich had never beheld there. He seemed fully sensible that he had done no small deed, and crossed a gulf separating tailors who put in linings, and execute repairs, from those who make new things. He took the cloak out of the pocket-handkerchief in which he had brought it. The handkerchief was fresh from the laundress, and he put it in his pocket for use. Taking out the cloak, he gazed proudly at it, held it up with both hands, and flung it skilfully over the shoulders of Akaky Akakiyevich. Then he pulled it and fitted it down behind with his hand, and he draped it around Akaky Akakiyevich without buttoning it. Akaky Akakiyevich, like an experienced man, wished to try the sleeves. Petrovich helped him on with them, and it turned out that the sleeves were satisfactory also. In short, the cloak appeared to be perfect, and most seasonable. Petrovich did not neglect to observe that it was only because he lived in a narrow street, and had no signboard, and had known Akaky Akakiyevich so long, that he had made it so cheaply; but that if he had been in business on the Nevsky Prospect, he would have charged seventy-five rubles for the making alone. Akaky Akakiyevich did not care to argue this point with Petrovich. He paid him, thanked him, and set out at once in his new cloak for the department. Petrovich followed him, and pausing in the street, gazed long at the cloak in the distance, after which he went to one side expressly to run through a crooked alley, and emerge again into the street beyond to gaze once more upon the cloak from another point, namely, directly in front.

Meantime Akaky Akakiyevich went on in holiday mood. He was conscious every second of the time that he had a new cloak on his shoulders, and several times he laughed with internal satisfaction. In fact, there were two advantages, one was its warmth, the other its beauty. He saw nothing of the road, but suddenly found himself at the department. He took off his cloak in the ante-room, looked it over carefully, and confided it to the special care of the attendant. It is impossible to say precisely how it was that every one in the department knew at once that Akaky Akakiyevich had a new cloak, and that the "cape" no longer existed. All rushed at the same moment into the ante-room to inspect it. They congratulated him, and said pleasant things to him, so that he began at first to smile, and then to grow ashamed. When all surrounded him, and said that the new cloak must be "christened," and that he must at least give them all a party, Akaky Akakiyevich lost his head completely, and did not know where he stood, what to answer, or how to get out of it. He stood blushing all over for several minutes, trying to assure them with great simplicity that it was not a new cloak, that it was in fact the old "cape."

At length one of the officials, assistant to the head clerk, in order to show that he was not at all proud, and on good terms with his inferiors, said:

"So be it, only I will give the party instead of Akaky Akakiyevich; I invite you all to tea with me to-night. It just happens to be my name-day too."

The officials naturally at once offered the assistant clerk their congratulations, and accepted the invitation with pleasure. Akaky Akakiyevich would have declined; but all declared that it was discourteous, that it was simply a sin and a shame, and that he could not possibly refuse. Besides, the notion became pleasant to him when he recollected that he should thereby have a chance of wearing his new cloak in the evening also.

That whole day was truly a most triumphant festival for Akaky Akakiyevich. He returned home in the most happy frame of mind, took off his cloak, and hung it carefully on the wall, admiring afresh the cloth and the lining. Then he brought out his old, worn-out cloak, for comparison. He looked at it, and laughed, so vast was the difference. And long after dinner he laughed again when the condition of the "cape" recurred to his mind. He dined cheerfully, and after dinner wrote nothing, but took his ease for a while on the bed, until it got dark. Then he dressed himself leisurely, put on his cloak, and stepped out into the street.

Where the host lived, unfortunately we cannot say. Our memory begins to fail us badly. The houses and streets in St. Petersburg have become so mixed up in our head that it is very difficult to get anything out of it again in proper form. This much is certain, that the official lived in the best part of the city; and therefore it must have been anything but near to Akaky Akakiyevich's residence. Akaky Akakiyevich was first obliged to traverse a kind of wilderness of deserted, dimly-lighted streets. But in proportion as he approached the official's quarter of the city, the streets became more lively, more populous, and more brilliantly illuminated. Pedestrians began to appear; handsomely dressed ladies were more frequently encountered; the men had otter skin collars to their coats; shabby sleigh-men with their wooden, railed sledges stuck over with brass-headed nails, became rarer; whilst on the other hand, more and more drivers in red velvet caps, lacquered sledges and bear-skin coats began to appear, and carriages with rich hammer-cloths flew swiftly through the streets, their wheels scrunching the snow.

Akaky Akakiyevich gazed upon all this as upon a novel sight. He had not been in the streets during the evening for years. He halted out of curiosity before a shop-window, to look at a picture representing a handsome woman, who had thrown off her shoe, thereby baring her whole foot in a very pretty way; whilst behind her the head of a man with whiskers and a handsome moustache peeped through the doorway of another room. Akaky Akakiyevich shook his head, and laughed, and then went on his way. Why did he laugh? Either because he had met with a thing utterly unknown, but for which every one cherishes, nevertheless, some sort of feeling, or else he thought, like many officials, "Well, those French! What is to be said? If they do go in for anything of that sort, why—" But possibly he did not think at all.

Akaky Akakiyevich at length reached the house in which the head clerk's assistant lodged. He lived in fine style. The staircase was lit by a lamp, his apartment being on the second floor. On entering the vestibule, Akaky Akakiyevich beheld a whole row of goloshes on the floor. Among them, in the centre of the room, stood a samovar, humming and emitting clouds of steam. On the walls hung all sorts of coats and cloaks, among which there were even some with beaver collars, or velvet facings. Beyond, the buzz of conversation was audible, and became clear and loud, when the servant came out with a trayful of empty glasses, cream-jugs and sugar-bowls. It was evident that the officials had arrived long before, and had already finished their first glass of tea.

Akaky Akakiyevich, having hung up his own cloak, entered the inner room. Before him all at once appeared lights, officials, pipes, and card-tables, and he was bewildered by a sound of rapid conversation rising from all the tables, and the noise of moving chairs. He halted very awkwardly in the middle of the room, wondering what he ought to do. But they had seen him. They received him with a shout, and all thronged at once into the ante-room, and there took another look at his cloak. Akaky Akakiyevich, although somewhat confused, was frank-hearted, and could not refrain from rejoicing when he saw how they praised his cloak. Then, of course, they all dropped him and his cloak, and returned, as was proper, to the tables set out for whist.

All this, the noise, the talk, and the throng of people, was rather overwhelming to Akaky Akakiyevich. He simply did not know where he stood, or where to put his hands, his feet, and his whole body. Finally he sat down by the players, looked at the cards, gazed at the face of one and another, and after a while began to gape, and to feel that it was wearisome, the more so, as the hour was already long past when he usually went to bed. He wanted to take leave of the host, but they would not let him go, saying that he must not fail to drink a glass of champagne, in honour of his new garment. In the course of an hour, supper, consisting of vegetable salad, cold veal, pastry, confectioner's pies, and champagne, was served. They made Akaky Akakiyevich drink two glasses of champagne, after which he felt things grow livelier.

Still, he could not forget that it was twelve o'clock, and that he should have been at home long ago. In order that the host might not think of some excuse for detaining him, he stole out of the room quickly, sought out, in the ante-room, his cloak, which, to his sorrow, he found lying on the floor, brushed it, picked off every speck upon it, put it on his shoulders, and descended the stairs to the street.

In the street all was still bright. Some petty shops, those permanent clubs of servants and all sorts of folks, were open. Others were shut, but, nevertheless, showed a streak of light the whole length of the door-crack, indicating that they were not yet free of company, and that probably some domestics, male and female, were finishing their stories and conversations, whilst leaving their masters in complete ignorance as to their whereabouts. Akaky Akakiyevich went on in a happy frame of mind. He even started to run, without knowing why, after some lady, who flew past like a flash of lightning. But he stopped short, and went on very quietly as before, wondering why he had quickened his pace. Soon there spread before him these deserted streets which are not cheerful in the daytime, to say no thing of the evening. Now they were even more dim and lonely. The lanterns began to grow rarer, oil, evidently, had been less liberally supplied. Then came wooden houses and fences. Not a soul anywhere; only the snow sparkled in the streets, and mournfully veiled the low-roofed cabins with their closed shutters. He approached the spot where the street crossed a vast square with houses barely visible on its farther side, a square which seemed a fearful desert.

Afar, a tiny spark glimmered from some watchman's-box, which seemed to stand on the edge of the world. Akaky Akakiyevich's cheerfulness diminished at this point in a marked degree. He entered the square, not without an involuntary sensation of fear, as though his heart warned him of some evil. He glanced back, and on both sides it was like a sea about him. "No, it is better not to look," he thought, and went on, closing his eyes. When he opened them, to see whether he was near the end of the square, he suddenly beheld, standing just before his very nose, some bearded individuals of precisely what sort, he could not make out. All grew dark before his eyes, and his heart throbbed.

"Of course, the cloak is mine!" said one of them in a loud voice, seizing hold of his collar. Akaky Akakiyevich was about to shout "Help!" when the second man thrust a fist, about the size of an official's head, at his very mouth, muttering, "Just you dare to scream!"

Akaky Akakiyevich felt them strip off his cloak, and give him a kick.

He fell headlong upon the snow, and felt no more.

In a few minutes he recovered consciousness, and rose to his feet, but no one was there. He felt that it was cold in the square, and that his cloak was gone. He began to shout, but his voice did not appear to reach the outskirts of the square. In despair, but without ceasing to shout, he started at a run across the square, straight towards the watch-box, beside which stood the watchman, leaning on his halberd, and apparently curious to know what kind of a customer was running towards him shouting. Akaky Akakiyevich ran up to him, and began in a sobbing voice to shout that he was asleep, and attended to nothing, and did not see when a man was robbed. The watchman replied that he had seen two men stop him in the middle of the square, but supposed that they were friends of his, and that, instead of scolding vainly, he had better go to the police on the morrow, so that they might make a search for whoever had stolen the cloak.

Akaky Akakiyevich ran home and arrived in a state of complete disorder, his hair which grew very thinly upon his temples and the back of his head all tousled, his body, arms and legs, covered with snow. The old woman, who was mistress of his lodgings, on hearing a terrible knocking, sprang hastily from her bed, and, with only one shoe on, ran to open the door, pressing the sleeve of her chemise to her bosom out of modesty. But when she had opened it, she fell back on beholding Akaky Akakiyevich in such a condition. When he told her about the affair, she clasped her hands, and said that he must go straight to the district chief of police, for his subordinate would turn up his nose, promise well, and drop the matter there. The very best thing to do, therefore, would be to go to the district chief, whom she knew, because Finnish Anna, her former cook, was now nurse at his house. She often saw him passing the house, and he was at church every Sunday, praying, but at the same time gazing cheerfully at everybody; so that he must be a good man, judging from all appearances. Having listened to this opinion, Akaky Akakiyevich betook himself sadly to his room. And how he spent the night there, any one who can put himself in another's place may readily imagine.

Early in the morning, he presented himself

at the district chief's, but was told the official was asleep. He went again at ten and was again informed that he was asleep. At eleven, and they said, "The superintendent is not at home." At dinner time, and the clerks in the ante-room would not admit him on any terms, and insisted upon knowing his business. So that at last, for once in his life, Akaky Akakiyevich felt an inclination to show some spirit, and said curtly that he must see the chief in person, that they ought not to presume to refuse him entrance, that he came from the department of justice, and that when he complained of them, they would see.

The clerks dared make no reply to this, and one of them went to call the chief, who listened to the strange story of the theft of the coat. Instead of directing his attention to the principal points of the matter, he began to question Akaky Akakiyevich. Why was he going home so late? Was he in the habit of doing so, or had he been to some disorderly house? So that Akaky Akakiyevich got thoroughly confused, and left him, without knowing whether the affair of his cloak was in proper train or not.

All that day, for the first time in his life, he

never went near the department. The next day he made his appearance, very pale, and in his old cape, which had become even more shabby. The news of the robbery of the cloak touched many, although there were some officials present who never lost an opportunity, even such a one as the present, of ridiculing Akaky Akakiyevich. They decided to make a collection for him on the spot, but the officials had already spent a great deal in subscribing for the director's portrait, and for some book, at the suggestion of the head of that division, who was a friend of the author; and so the sum was trifling.

One of them, moved by pity, resolved to help Akaky Akakiyevich with some good advice, at least, and told him that he ought not to go to the police, for although it might happen that a police-officer, wishing to win the approval of his superiors, might hunt up the cloak by some means, still, his cloak would remain in the possession of the police if he did not offer legal proof that it belonged to him. The best thing for him, therefore, would be to apply to a certain prominent personage; since this prominent personage, by entering into relation with the proper persons, could greatly expedite the matter.

As there was nothing else to be done, Akaky Akakiyevich decided to go to the prominent personage. What was the exact official position of the prominent personage, remains unknown to this day. The reader must know that the prominent personage had but recently become a prominent personage, having up to that time been only an insignificant person. Moreover, his present position was not considered prominent in comparison with others still more so. But there is always a circle of people to whom what is insignificant in the eyes of others, is important enough. Moreover, he strove to increase his importance by sundry devices. For instance, he managed to have the inferior officials meet him on the staircase when he entered upon his service; no one was to presume to come directly to him, but the strictest etiquette must be observed; the collegiate recorder must make a report to the government secretary, the government secretary to the titular councillor, or whatever other man was proper, and all business must come before him in this manner. In Holy Russia, all is thus contaminated with the love of imitation; every man imitates and copies his superior. They even say that a certain titular councillor, when promoted to the head of some small separate office, immediately partitioned off a private room for himself, called it the audience chamber, and posted at the door a lackey with red collar and braid, who grasped the handle of the door, and opened to all comers, though the audience chamber would hardly hold an ordinary writing table.

The manners and customs of the prominent personage were grand and imposing, but rather exaggerated. The main foundation of his system was strictness. "Strictness, strictness, and always strictness!" he generally said; and at the last word he looked significantly into the face of the person to whom he spoke. But there was no necessity for this, for the halfscore of subordinates, who formed the entire force of the office, were properly afraid. On catching sight of him afar off, they left their work, and waited, drawn up in line, until he had passed through the room. His ordinary converse with his inferiors smacked of sternness, and consisted chiefly of three phrases: "How dare you?" "Do you know whom you are speaking to?" "Do you realise who is standing before you?"

Otherwise he was a very kind-hearted man, good to his comrades, and ready to oblige.

But the rank of general threw him completely off his balance. On receiving any one of that rank, he became confused, lost his way, as it were, and never knew what to do. If he chanced to be amongst his equals, he was still a very nice kind of man, a very good fellow in many respects, and not stupid, but the very moment that he found himself in the society of people but one rank lower than himself, he became silent. And his situation aroused sympathy, the more so, as he felt himself that he might have been making an incomparably better use of his time. In his eyes, there was sometimes visible a desire to join some interesting conversation or group, but he was kept back by the thought, "Would it not be a very great condescension on his part? Would it not be familiar? And would he not thereby lose his importance?" And in consequence of such reflections, he always remained in the same dumb state, uttering from time to time a few monosyllabic sounds, and thereby earning the name of the most wearisome of men.

To this prominent personage Akaky Akakiyevich presented himself, and this at the most unfavourable time for himself, though opportune for the prominent personage. The prominent personage was in his cabinet, conversing very gaily with an old acquaintance and companion of his childhood, whom he had not seen for several years, and who had just arrived, when it was announced to him that a person named Bashmachkin had come. He asked abruptly, "Who is he?"—"Some official," he was informed. "Ah, he can wait! This is no time for him to call," said the important man.

It must be remarked here that the important man lied outrageously. He had said all he had to say to his friend long before, and the conversation had been interspersed for some time with very long pauses, during which they merely slapped each other on the leg, and said, "You think so, Ivan Abramovich!" "Just so, Stepan Varlamovich!" Nevertheless, he ordered that the official should be kept waiting, in order to show his friend, a man who had not been in the service for a long time, but had lived at home in the country, how long officials had to wait in his ante-room.

At length, having talked himself completely out, and more than that, having had his fill of pauses, and smoked a cigar in a very comfortable arm-chair with reclining back, he suddenly seemed to recollect, and said to the secretary, who stood by the door with papers of reports, "So it seems that there is an official waiting to see me. Tell him that he may come in." On perceiving Akaky Akakiyevich's modest mien and his worn uniform, he turned abruptly to him, and said, "What do you want?" in a curt hard voice, which he had practised in his room in private, and before the looking-glass, for a whole week before being raised to his present rank.

Akaky Akakiyevich, who was already imbued with a due amount of fear, became somewhat confused, and as well as his tongue would permit, explained, with a rather more frequent addition than usual of the word "that" that his cloak was quite new, and had been stolen in the most inhuman manner; that he had applied to him, in order that he might, in some way, by his intermediation—that he might enter into correspondence with the chief of police, and find the cloak.

For some inexplicable reason, this conduct seemed familiar to the prominent personage.

"What, my dear sir!" he said abruptly, "are you not acquainted with etiquette? To whom have you come? Don't you know how such matters are managed? You should first have presented a petition to the office. It would have gone to the head of the department, then to the chief of the division, then it would have been handed over to the secretary, and the secretary would have given it to me."

"But, your excellency," said Akaky Akakiyevich, trying to collect his small handful of wits, and conscious at the same time that he was perspiring terribly, "I, your excellency, presumed to trouble you because secretaries—are an untrustworthy race."

"What, what, what!" said the important personage. "Where did you get such courage? Where did you get such ideas? What impudence towards their chiefs and superiors has spread among the young generation!" The prominent personage apparently had not observed that Akaky Akakiyevich was already in the neighbourhood of fifty. If he could be called a young man, it must have been in comparison with some one who was seventy. "Do you know to whom you are speaking? Do you realise who is standing before you? Do you realise it? Do you realise it, I ask you!" Then he stamped his foot, and raised his voice to such a pitch that it would have frightened even a different man from Akaky Akakiyevich.

Akaky Akakiyevich's senses failed him. He staggered, trembled in every limb, and, if the porters had not run in to support him, would have fallen to the floor. They carried him out insensible. But the prominent personage, gratified that the effect should have surpassed his expectations, and quite intoxicated with the thought that his word could even deprive a man of his senses, glanced sideways at his friend in order to see how he looked upon this, and perceived, not without satisfaction, that his friend was in a most uneasy frame of mind, and even beginning on his part, to feel a trifle frightened.

Akaky Akakiyevich could not remember how he descended the stairs, and got into the street. He felt neither his hands nor feet. Never in his life had he been so rated by any high official, let alone a strange one. He went staggering on through the snow-storm, which was blowing in the streets, with his mouth wide open. The wind, in St. Petersburg fashion, darted upon him from all quarters, and down every cross-street. In a twinkling it had blown a quinsy into his throat, and he reached home unable to utter a word. His throat was swollen, and he lay down on his bed. So powerful is sometimes a good scolding!

The next day a violent fever developed. Thanks to the generous assistance of the St. Petersburg climate, the malady progressed more rapidly than could have been expected, and when the doctor arrived, he found, on feeling the sick man's pulse, that there was nothing to be done, except to prescribe a poultice, so that the patient might not be left entirely without the beneficent aid of medicine. But at the same time, he predicted his end in thirty-six hours. After this he turned to the landlady, and said, "And as for you, don't waste your time on him. Order his pine coffin now, for an oak one will be too expensive for him."

Did Akaky Akakiyevich hear these fatal words? And if he heard them, did they produce any overwhelming effect upon him? Did he lament the bitterness of his life?—We know not, for he continued in a delirious condition. Visions incessantly appeared to him, each stranger than the other. Now he saw Petrovich, and ordered him to make a cloak, with some traps for robbers, who seemed to him to be always under the bed; and he cried every moment to the landlady to pull one of them from under his coverlet. Then he inquired why his old mantle hung before him when he had a new cloak. Next he fancied that he was standing before the prominent person, listening to a thorough setting-down and saying, "Forgive me, your excellency!" but at last he began to curse, uttering the most horrible words, so that his aged landlady crossed herself, never in her life having heard anything of the kind from him, and more so as these words followed directly after the words "your excellency." Later on he talked utter nonsense, of which nothing could be made, all that was evident being that these incoherent words and thoughts hovered ever about one thing, his cloak.

At length poor Akaky Akakiyevich breathed his last. They sealed up neither his room nor his effects, because, in the first place, there were no heirs, and, in the second, there was very little to inherit beyond a bundle of goose-quills, a quire of white official paper, three pairs of socks, two or three buttons which had burst off his trousers, and the mantle already known to the reader. To whom all this fell, God knows. I confess that the person who told me this tale took no interest in the matter. They carried Akaky Akakiyevich out, and buried him.

And St. Petersburg was left without Akaky Akakiyevich, as though he had never lived there. A being disappeared, who was protected by none, dear to none, interesting to none, and who never even attracted to himself the attention of those students of human nature who omit no opportunity of thrusting a pin through a common fly and examining it under the microscope. A being who bore meekly the jibes of the department, and went to his grave without having done one unusual deed, but to whom, nevertheless, at the close of his life, appeared a bright visitant in the form of a cloak, which momentarily cheered his poor life, and upon him, thereafter, an intolerable misfortune descended, just as it descends upon the heads of the mighty of this world!

Several days after his death, the porter was sent from the department to his lodgings, with an order for him to present himself there immediately, the chief commanding it. But the porter had to return unsuccessful, with the answer that he could not come; and to the question, "Why?" replied, "Well, because he is dead! he was buried four days ago." In this manner did they hear of Akaky Akakiyevich's death at the department. And the next day a new official sat in his place, with a handwriting by no means so upright, but more inclined and slanting.

But who could have imagined that this was not really the end of Akaky Akakiyevich, that he was destined to raise a commotion after death, as if in compensation for his utterly insignificant life? But so it happened, and our poor story unexpectedly gains a fantastic ending.

A rumour suddenly spread through St. Petersburg, that a dead man had taken to appearing on the Kalinkin Bridge, and its vicinity, at night in the form of an official seeking a stolen cloak, and that, under the pretext of its being the stolen cloak, he dragged, without regard to rank or calling, every one's cloak from his shoulders, be it cat-skin, beaver, fox, bear, sable, in a word, every sort of fur and skin which men adopted for their covering. One of the department officials saw the dead man with his own eyes, and immediately recognised in him Akaky Akakiyevich. This, however, inspired him with such terror, that he ran off with all his might, and therefore did not scan the dead man closely, but only saw how the latter threatened him from afar with his finger. Constant complaints poured in from all quarters, that the backs and shoulders, not only of titular but even of court councillors, were exposed to the danger of a cold, on account of the frequent dragging off of their cloaks.

Arrangements were made by the police to catch the corpse, alive or dead, at any cost, and punish him as an example to others, in the most severe manner. In this they nearly succeeded, for a watchman, on guard in Kirinshkin Lane, caught the corpse by the collar on the very scene of his evil deeds, when attempting to pull off the frieze cloak of a retired musician. Having seized him by the collar, he summoned, with a shout, two of his comrades, whom he enjoined to hold him fast, while he himself felt for a moment in his boot, in order to draw out his snuff-box, and refresh his frozen nose. But the snuff was of a sort which even a corpse could not endure. The watchman having closed his right nostril with his finger, had no sooner succeeded in holding half a handful up to the left, than the corpse sneezed so violently that he completely filled the eyes of all three. While they raised their hands to wipe them, the dead man vanished completely, so that they positively did not know whether they had actually had him in their grip at all. Thereafter the watchmen conceived such a terror of dead men that they were afraid even to seize the living, and only screamed from a distance. "Hey, there! go your way!" So the dead official began to appear even beyond the Kalinkin Bridge, causing no little terror to all timid people.

But we have totally neglected that certain prominent personage who may really be considered as the cause of the fantastic turn taken by this true history. First of all, justice compels us to say, that after the departure of poor, annihilated Akaky Akakiyevich, he felt something like remorse. Suffering was unpleasant to him, for his heart was accessible to many good impulses, in spite of the fact that his rank often prevented his showing his true self. As soon as his friend had left his cabinet, he began to think about poor Akaky Akakiyevich. And from that day forth, poor Akaky Akakiyevich, who could not bear up under an official reprimand, recurred to his mind almost every day. The thought troubled him to such an extent, that a week later he even resolved to send an official to him, to learn whether he really could assist him. And when it was reported to him that Akaky Akakiyevich had died suddenly of fever, he was startled, hearkened to the reproaches of his conscience, and was out of sorts for the whole day.

Wishing to divert his mind in some way and drive away the disagreeable impression, he set out that evening for one of his friends' houses, where he found quite a large party assembled. What was better, nearly every one was of the same rank as himself, so that he need not feel in the least constrained. This had a marvellous effect upon his mental state. He grew expansive, made himself agreeable in conversation, in short, he passed a delightful evening. After supper he drank a couple of glasses of champagne—not a bad recipe for cheerfulness, as every one knows. The champagne inclined him to various adventures, and he determined not to return home, but to go and see a certain well-known lady, of German extraction, Karolina Ivanovna, a lady, it appears, with whom he was on a very friendly footing.

It must be mentioned that the prominent

personage was no longer a young man, but a good husband and respected father of a family. Two sons, one of whom was already in the service, and a good-looking, sixteen-year-old daughter, with a slightly arched but pretty little nose, came every morning to kiss his hand and say, "Bon jour, papa." His wife, a still fresh and good-looking woman, first gave him her hand to kiss, and then, reversing the procedure, kissed his. But the prominent personage, though perfectly satisfied in his domestic relations, considered it stylish to have a friend in another quarter of the city. This friend was scarcely prettier or younger than his wife; but there are such puzzles in the world, and it is not our place to judge them. So the important personage descended the stairs, stepped into his sledge, said to the coachman, "To Karolina Ivanovna's," and, wrapping himself luxuriously in his warm cloak, found himself in that delightful frame of mind than which a Russian can conceive nothing better, namely, when you think of nothing yourself, yet when the thoughts creep into your mind of their own accord, each more agreeable than the other, giving you no trouble either to drive them away, or seek them. Fully satisfied, he recalled all the gay features of the evening just passed and all the mots which had made the little circle laugh. Many of them he repeated in a low voice, and found them quite as funny as before; so it is not surprising that he should laugh heartily at them. Occasionally, however, he was interrupted by gusts of wind, which, coming suddenly, God knows whence or why, cut his face, drove masses of snow into it, filled out his cloak-collar like a sail, or suddenly blew it over his head with supernatural force, and thus caused him constant trouble to disentangle himself.

Suddenly the important personage felt some one clutch him firmly by the collar. Turning round, he perceived a man of short stature, in an old, worn uniform, and recognised, not without terror, Akaky Akakiyevich. The official's face was white as snow, and looked just like a corpse's. But the horror of the important personage transcended all bounds when he saw the dead man's mouth open, and heard it utter the following remarks, while it breathed upon him the terrible odour of the grave: "Ah, here you are at last! I have you, that—by the collar! I need your cloak. You took no trouble about mine, but reprimanded me. So now give up your own."

The pallid prominent personage almost

died of fright. Brave as he was in the office and in the presence of inferiors generally, and although, at the sight of his manly form and appearance, every one said, "Ugh! how much character he has!" at this crisis, he, like many possessed of an heroic exterior, experienced such terror, that, not without cause, he began to fear an attack of illness. He flung his cloak hastily from his shoulders and shouted to his coachman in an unnatural voice, "Home at full speed!" The coachman, hearing the tone which is generally employed at critical moments, and even accompanied by something much more tangible, drew his head down between his shoulders in case of an emergency, flourished his whip, and flew on like an arrow. In a little more than six minutes the prominent personage was at the entrance of his own house. Pale, thoroughly scared, and cloakless, he went home instead of to Karolina Ivanovna's, reached his room somehow or other, and passed the night in the direst distress; so that the next morning over their tea, his daughter said, "You are very pale to-day, papa." But papa remained silent, and said not a word to any one of what had happened to him, where he had been, or where he had intended to go.

This occurrence made a deep impression upon him. He even began to say, "How dare you? Do you realise who is standing before you?" less frequently to the under-officials, and, if he did utter the words, it was only after first having learned the bearings of the matter. But the most noteworthy point was, that from that day forward the apparition of the dead official ceased to be seen. Evidently the prominent personage's cloak just fitted his shoulders. At all events, no more instances of his dragging cloaks from people's shoulders were heard of. But many active and solicitous persons could by no means reassure themselves, and asserted that the dead official still showed himself in distant parts of the city.

In fact, one watchman in Kolomen saw with his own eyes the apparition come from behind a house. But the watchman was not a strong man, so he was afraid to arrest him, and followed him in the dark, until, at length, the apparition looked round, paused, and inquired, "What do you want?" at the same time showing such a fist as is never seen on living men. The watchman said, "Nothing," and turned back instantly. But the apparition was much too tall, wore huge moustaches, and, directing its steps apparently towards the

Obukhov Bridge, disappeared in the darkness of the night.

THE CHRISTMAS TREE AND THE WEDDING

BY FIODOR M. DOSTOYEVSKY

The other day I saw a wedding... But no! I would rather tell you about a Christmas tree. The wedding was superb. I liked it immensely. But the other incident was still finer. I don't know why it is that the sight of the wedding reminded me of the Christmas tree. This is the way it happened:

Exactly five years ago, on New Year's Eve, I was invited to a children's ball by a man high up in the business world, who had his connections, his circle of acquaintances, and his intrigues. So it seemed as though the children's ball was merely a pretext for the parents to come together and discuss matters of interest to themselves, quite innocently and casually.

I was an outsider, and, as I had no special matters to air, I was able to spend the evening independently of the others. There was another gentleman present who like myself had just stumbled upon this affair of domestic bliss. He was the first to attract my attention. His appearance was not that of a man of birth or high family. He was tall, rather thin, very serious, and well dressed. Apparently he had no heart for the family festivities. The instant he went off into a corner by himself the smile disappeared from his face, and his thick dark brows knitted into a frown. He knew no one except the host and showed every sign of being bored to death, though bravely sustaining the role of thorough enjoyment to the end. Later I learned that he was a provincial, had come to the capital on some important, brain-racking business, had brought a letter of recommendation to our host, and our host had taken him under his protection, not at all con amore. It was merely out of politeness that he had invited him to the children's ball.

They did not play cards with him, they did not offer him cigars. No one entered into conversation with him. Possibly they recognised the bird by its feathers from a distance. Thus, my gentleman, not knowing what to do with his hands, was compelled to spend the evening stroking his whiskers. His whiskers were really fine, but he stroked them so assiduously that one got the feeling that the whiskers had come into the world first and afterwards the man in order to stroke them.

There was another guest who interested me. But he was of quite a different order. He was a personage. They called him Julian Mastakovich. At first glance one could tell he was an honoured guest and stood in the same relation to the host as the host to the gentleman of the whiskers. The host and hostess said no end of amiable things to him, were most attentive, wining him, hovering over him, bringing guests up to be introduced, but never leading him to any one else. I noticed tears glisten in our host's eyes when Julian Mastakovich remarked that he had rarely spent such a pleasant evening. Somehow I began to feel uncomfortable in this personage's presence. So, after amusing myself with the children, five of whom, remarkably well-fed young persons, were our host's, I went into a little sitting-room, entirely unoccupied, and seated myself at the end that was a conservatory and took up almost half the room.

The children were charming. They absolutely refused to resemble their elders, notwithstanding the efforts of mothers and governesses. In a jiffy they had denuded the Christmas tree down to the very last sweet and had already succeeded in breaking half of their playthings before they even found out which belonged to whom.

One of them was a particularly handsome little lad, dark-eyed, curly-haired, who stubbornly persisted in aiming at me with his wooden gun. But the child that attracted the greatest attention was his sister, a girl of about eleven, lovely as a Cupid. She was quiet and thoughtful, with large, full, dreamy eyes. The children had somehow offended her, and she left them and walked into the same room that I had withdrawn into. There she seated herself with her doll in a corner.

"Her father is an immensely wealthy business man," the guests informed each other in tones of awe. "Three hundred thousand rubles set aside for her dowry already."

As I turned to look at the group from which

I heard this news item issuing, my glance met Julian Mastakovich's. He stood listening to the insipid chatter in an attitude of concentrated attention, with his hands behind his back and his head inclined to one side.

All the while I was quite lost in admiration of the shrewdness our host displayed in the dispensing of the gifts. The little maid of the many-rubied dowry received the handsomest doll, and the rest of the gifts were graded in value according to the diminishing scale of the parents' stations in life. The last child, a tiny chap of ten, thin, red-haired, freckled, came into possession of a small book of nature stories without illustrations or even head and tail pieces. He was the governess's child. She was a poor widow, and her little boy, clad in a sorry-looking little nankeen jacket, looked thoroughly crushed and intimidated. He took the book of nature stories and circled slowly about the children's toys. He would have given anything to play with them. But he did not dare to. You could tell he already knew his place.

I like to observe children. It is fascinating to watch the individuality in them struggling for self-assertion. I could see that the other children's things had tremendous charm for the red-haired boy, especially a toy theatre, in which he was so anxious to take a part that he resolved to fawn upon the other children. He smiled and began to play with them. His one and only apple he handed over to a puffy urchin whose pockets were already crammed with sweets, and he even carried another youngster pickaback—all simply that he might be allowed to stay with the theatre.

But in a few moments an impudent young person fell on him and gave him a pummelling. He did not dare even to cry. The governess came and told him to leave off interfering with the other children's games, and he crept away to the same room the little girl and I were in. She let him sit down beside her, and the two set themselves busily dressing the expensive doll.

Almost half an hour passed, and I was nearly dozing off, as I sat there in the conservatory half listening to the chatter of the red-haired boy and the dowered beauty, when Julian Mastakovich entered suddenly. He had slipped out of the drawing-room under cover of a noisy scene among the children. From my secluded corner it had not escaped my notice that a few moments before he had been eagerly conversing with the rich girl's father, to whom he had only just been introduced.

He stood still for a while reflecting and mumbling to himself, as if counting something on his fingers.

"Three hundred—three hundred—eleven—twelve—thirteen—sixteen—in five years! Let's say four per cent—five times twelve—sixty, and on these sixty——. Let us assume that in five years it will amount to—well, four hundred. Hm—hm! But the shrewd old fox isn't likely to be satisfied with four per cent. He gets eight or even ten, perhaps. Let's suppose five hundred, five hundred thousand, at least, that's sure. Anything above that for pocket money—hm—"

He blew his nose and was about to leave the room when he spied the girl and stood still. I, behind the plants, escaped his notice. He seemed to me to be quivering with excitement. It must have been his calculations that upset him so. He rubbed his hands and danced from place to place, and kept getting more and more excited. Finally, however, he conquered his emotions and came to a standstill. He cast a determined look at the future bride and wanted to move toward her, but glanced about first. Then, as if with a guilty conscience, he stepped over to the child on tip-toe, smiling, and bent down and kissed her head.

His coming was so unexpected that she uttered a shriek of alarm.

"What are you doing here, dear child?" he whispered, looking around and pinching her cheek.

"We're playing."

"What, with him?" said Julian Mastakovich with a look askance at the governess's child. "You should go into the drawing-room, my lad," he said to him.

The boy remained silent and looked up at the man with wide-open eyes. Julian Mastakovich glanced round again cautiously and bent down over the girl.

"What have you got, a doll, my dear?"

"Yes, sir." The child quailed a little, and her

brow wrinkled.

"A doll? And do you know, my dear, what dolls are made of?"

"No, sir," she said weakly, and lowered her head.

"Out of rags, my dear. You, boy, you go back to the drawing-room, to the children," said Julian Mastakovich looking at the boy sternly.

The two children frowned. They caught hold of each other and would not part.

"And do you know why they gave you the doll?" asked Julian
Mastakovich, dropping his voice lower and lower.
"No."

"Because you were a good, very good little girl the whole week."

Saying which, Julian Mastakovich was seized with a paroxysm of agitation. He looked round and said in a tone faint, almost inaudible with excitement and impatience:

"If I come to visit your parents will you love me, my dear?"

He tried to kiss the sweet little creature, but the red-haired boy saw that she was on the verge of tears, and he caught her hand and sobbed out loud in sympathy. That enraged the man.

"Go away! Go away! Go back to the other room, to your playmates."

"I don't want him to. I don't want him to! You go away!" cried the girl. "Let him alone! Let him alone!" She was almost weeping.

There was a sound of footsteps in the door-way. Julian Mastakovich started and straight-ened up his respectable body. The red-haired boy was even more alarmed. He let go the girl's hand, sidled along the wall, and escaped through the drawing-room into the dining-room.

Not to attract attention, Julian Mastakovich also made for the dining-room. He was red as a lobster. The sight of himself in a mirror seemed to embarrass him. Presumably he was annoyed at his own ardour and impatience. Without due respect to his importance and dignity, his calculations had lured and pricked him to the greedy eagerness of a boy, who makes straight for his object—though this was not as yet an object; it only would be so in five years' time. I followed the worthy man into the dining-room, where I witnessed a remarkable play.

Julian Mastakovich, all flushed with vexation, venom in his look, began to threaten the red-haired boy. The red-haired boy retreated farther and farther until there was no place left for him to retreat to, and he did not know where to turn in his fright.

"Get out of here! What are you doing here? Get out, I say, you good-for-nothing! Stealing fruit, are you? Oh, so, stealing fruit! Get out, you freckle face, go to your likes!"

The frightened child, as a last desperate resort, crawled quickly under the table. His persecutor, completely infuriated, pulled out his large linen handkerchief and used it as a lash to drive the boy out of his position.

Here I must remark that Julian Mastakovich was a somewhat corpulent man, heavy, well-fed, puffy-cheeked, with a paunch and ankles as round as nuts. He perspired and puffed and panted. So strong was his dislike (or was it jealousy?) of the child that he actually began to carry on like a madman.

I laughed heartily. Julian Mastakovich turned. He was utterly confused and for a moment, apparently, quite oblivious of his immense importance. At that moment our host appeared in the doorway opposite. The boy crawled out from under the table and wiped his knees and elbows. Julian Mastakovich hastened to carry his handkerchief, which he had been dangling by the corner, to his nose. Our host looked at the three of us rather suspiciously. But, like a man who knows the world and can readily adjust himself, he seized upon the opportunity to lay hold of his very valuable guest and get what he wanted out of him.

"Here's the boy I was talking to you about," he said, indicating the red-haired child. "I took the liberty of presuming on your goodness in his behalf."

"Oh," replied Julian Mastakovich, still not

quite master of himself.

"He's my governess's son," our host continued in a beseeching tone. "She's a poor creature, the widow of an honest official. That's why, if it were possible for you—"

"Impossible, impossible!" Julian Mastakovich cried hastily. "You must excuse me, Philip Alexeyevich, I really cannot. I've made inquiries. There are no vacancies, and there is a waiting list of ten who have a greater right—I'm sorry."

"Too bad," said our host. "He's a quiet, unobtrusive child."

"A very naughty little rascal, I should say," said Julian Mastakovich, wryly. "Go away, boy. Why are you here still? Be off with you to the other children."

Unable to control himself, he gave me a sidelong glance. Nor could I control myself. I laughed straight in his face. He turned away and asked our host, in tones quite audible to me, who that odd young fellow was. They whispered to each other and left the room, disregarding me.

I shook with laughter. Then I, too, went to the drawing-room. There the great man, already surrounded by the fathers and mothers and the host and the hostess, had begun to talk eagerly with a lady to whom he had just been introduced. The lady held the rich little girl's hand. Julian Mastakovich went into fulsome praise of her. He waxed ecstatic over the dear child's beauty, her talents, her grace, her excellent breeding, plainly laying himself out to flatter the mother, who listened scarcely able to restrain tears of joy, while the father showed his delight by a gratified smile.

The joy was contagious. Everybody shared in it. Even the children were obliged to stop playing so as not to disturb the conversation. The atmosphere was surcharged with awe. I heard the mother of the important little girl, touched to her profoundest depths, ask Julian Mastakovich in the choicest language of courtesy, whether he would honour them by coming to see them. I heard Julian Mastakovich accept the invitation with unfeigned enthusiasm. Then the guests scattered decorously to different parts of the room, and I heard them, with veneration in their tones, extol the business man, the business man's wife, the business man's daughter, and, especially, Julian Mastakovich.

"Is he married?" I asked out loud of an acquaintance of mine standing beside Julian Mastakovich.

Julian Mastakovich gave me a venomous look.

"No," answered my acquaintance, profoundly shocked by my—intentional—indiscretion.

* * * * *

Not long ago I passed the Church of——. I was struck by the concourse of people gathered there to witness a wedding. It was a dreary day. A drizzling rain was beginning to come down. I made my way through the throng into the church. The bridegroom was a round, well-fed, pot-bellied little man, very much dressed up. He ran and fussed about and gave orders and arranged things. Finally word was passed that the bride was coming. I pushed through the crowd, and I beheld a marvellous beauty whose first spring was scarcely commencing. But the beauty was pale and sad. She looked distracted. It seemed to me even that her eyes were red from recent weeping. The classic severity of every line of her face imparted a peculiar significance and solemnity to her beauty. But through that severity and solemnity, through the sadness, shone the innocence of a child. There was something inexpressibly naïve, unsettled and young in her features, which, without words, seemed to plead for mercy.

They said she was just sixteen years old. I looked at the bridegroom carefully. Suddenly I recognised Julian Mastakovich, whom I had not seen again in all those five years. Then I looked at the bride again.—Good God! I made my way, as quickly as I could, out of the church. I heard gossiping in the crowd about the bride's wealth—about her dowry of five hundred thousand rubles—so and so much for pocket money.

"Then his calculations were correct," I thought, as I pressed out into the street.

THE DARLING

BY ANTON P. CHEKHOV

Olenka, the daughter of the retired collegiate assessor Plemyanikov, was sitting on the back-door steps of her house doing nothing. It was hot, the flies were nagging and teasing, and it was pleasant to think that it would soon be evening. Dark rain clouds were gathering from the east, wafting a breath of moisture every now and then.

Kukin, who roomed in the wing of the same house, was standing in the yard looking up at the sky. He was the manager of the Tivoli, an open-air theatre.

"Again," he said despairingly. "Rain again. Rain, rain, rain! Every day rain! As though to spite me. I might as well stick my head into a noose and be done with it. It's ruining me. Heavy losses every day!" He wrung his hands, and continued, addressing Olenka: "What a life, Olga Semyonovna! It's enough to make a man weep. He works, he does his best, his very best, he tortures himself, he passes sleepless nights, he thinks and thinks and thinks how to do everything just right. And what's the result? He gives the public the best operetta, the very best pantomime, excellent artists. But do they want it? Have they the least appreciation of it? The public is rude. The public is a great boor. The public wants a circus, a lot of nonsense, a lot of stuff. And there's the weather. Look! Rain almost every evening. It began to rain on the tenth of May, and it's kept it up through the whole of June. It's simply awful. I can't get any audiences, and don't I have to pay rent? Don't I have to pay the actors?"

The next day towards evening the clouds gathered again, and Kukin said with an hysterical laugh:

"Oh, I don't care. Let it do its worst. Let it drown the whole theatre, and me, too. All right, no luck for me in this world or the next. Let the actors bring suit against me and drag me to court. What's the court? Why not Siberia at hard labour, or even the scaffold? Ha, ha, ha!"

It was the same on the third day.

Olenka listened to Kukin seriously, in silence. Sometimes tears would rise to her eyes. At last Kukin's misfortune touched her. She fell in love with him. He was short, gaunt, with a yellow face, and curly hair combed back from his forehead, and a thin tenor voice. His features puckered all up when he spoke. Despair was ever inscribed on his face. And yet he awakened in Olenka a sincere, deep feeling.

She was always loving somebody. She couldn't get on without loving somebody. She had loved her sick father, who sat the whole time in his armchair in a darkened room, breathing heavily. She had loved her aunt, who came from Brianska once or twice a year to visit them. And before that, when a pupil at the progymnasium, she had loved her French teacher. She was a quiet, kind-hearted, compassionate girl, with a soft gentle way about her. And she made a very healthy, wholesome impression. Looking at her full, rosy cheeks, at her soft white neck with the black mole, and at the good naïve smile that always played on her face when something pleasant was said, the men would think, "Not so bad," and would smile too; and the lady visitors, in the middle of the conversation, would suddenly grasp her hand and exclaim, "You darling!" in a burst of delight.

The house, hers by inheritance, in which she had lived from birth, was located at the outskirts of the city on the Gypsy Road, not far from the Tivoli. From early evening till late at night she could hear the music in the theatre and the bursting of the rockets; and it seemed to her that Kukin was roaring and battling with his fate and taking his chief enemy, the indifferent public, by assault. Her heart melted softly, she felt no desire to sleep, and when Kukin returned home towards morning, she tapped on her window-pane, and through the curtains he saw her face and one shoulder and the kind smile she gave him.

He proposed to her, and they were married. And when he had a good look of her neck and her full vigorous shoulders, he clapped his hands and said:

"You darling!"

He was happy. But it rained on their wedding-day, and the expression of despair never left his face.

They got along well together. She sat in the cashier's box, kept the theatre in order, wrote down the expenses, and paid out the salaries. Her rosy cheeks, her kind naïve smile, like a halo around her face, could be seen at the cashier's window, behind the scenes, and in the café. She began to tell her friends that the theatre was the greatest, the most important, the most essential thing in the world, that it was the only place to obtain true enjoyment in and become humanised and educated.

"But do you suppose the public appreciates it?" she asked. "What the public wants is the circus. Yesterday Vanichka and I gave Faust Burlesqued, and almost all the boxes were empty. If we had given some silly nonsense, I assure you, the theatre would have been overcrowded. To-morrow we'll put Orpheus in Hades on. Do come."

Whatever Kukin said about the theatre and the actors, she repeated. She spoke, as he did, with contempt of the public, of its indifference to art, of its boorishness. She meddled in the rehearsals, corrected the actors, watched the conduct of the musicians; and when an unfavourable criticism appeared in the local paper, she wept and went to the editor to argue with him.

The actors were fond of her and called her "Vanichka and I" and "the darling." She was sorry for them and lent them small sums. When they bilked her, she never complained to her husband; at the utmost she shed a few tears.

In winter, too, they got along nicely together. They leased a theatre in the town for the whole winter and sublet it for short periods to a Little Russian theatrical company, to a conjuror and to the local amateur players.

Olenka grew fuller and was always beaming with contentment; while Kukin grew thinner and yellower and complained of his terrible losses, though he did fairly well the whole winter. At night he coughed, and she gave him raspberry syrup and lime water, rubbed him with eau de Cologne, and wrapped him up in soft coverings.

"You are my precious sweet," she said with

perfect sincerity, stroking his hair. "You are such a dear."

At Lent he went to Moscow to get his company together, and, while without him, Olenka was unable to sleep. She sat at the window the whole time, gazing at the stars. She likened herself to the hens that are also uneasy and unable to sleep when their rooster is out of the coop. Kukin was detained in Moscow. He wrote he would be back during Easter Week, and in his letters discussed arrangements already for the Tivoli. But late one night, before Easter Monday, there was an ill-omened knocking at the wicket-gate. It was like a knocking on a barrel—boom, boom, boom! The sleepy cook ran barefooted, plashing through the puddles, to open the gate.

"Open the gate, please," said some one in a hollow bass voice. "I have a telegram for you."

Olenka had received telegrams from her husband before; but this time, somehow, she was numbed with terror. She opened the telegram with trembling hands and read:

"Ivan Petrovich died suddenly to-day. Awaiting propt orders for wuneral Tuesday."

That was the way the telegram was written—"wuneral"—and another unintelligible word—"propt." The telegram was signed by the manager of the opera company.

"My dearest!" Olenka burst out sobbing. "Vanichka, my dearest, my sweetheart. Why did I ever meet you? Why did I ever get to know you and love you? To whom have you abandoned your poor Olenka, your poor, unhappy Olenka?"

Kukin was buried on Tuesday in the Vagankov Cemetery in Moscow. Olenka returned home on Wednesday; and as soon as she entered her house she threw herself on her bed and broke into such loud sobbing that she could be heard in the street and in the neighbouring yards.

"The darling!" said the neighbours, crossing themselves. "How Olga

Semyonovna, the poor darling, is grieving!"

Three months afterwards Olenka was returning home from mass, downhearted and in deep mourning. Beside her walked a man also returning from church, Vasily Pustovalov, the manager of the merchant Babakayev's lumber-yard. He was wearing a straw hat, a white vest with a gold chain, and looked more like a landowner than a business man.

"Everything has its ordained course, Olga Semyonovna," he said sedately, with sympathy in his voice. "And if any one near and dear to us dies, then it means it was God's will and we should remember that and bear it with submission."

He took her to the wicket-gate, said good-bye and went away. After that she heard his sedate voice the whole day; and on closing her eyes she instantly had a vision of his dark beard. She took a great liking to him. And evidently he had been impressed by her, too; for, not long after, an elderly woman, a distant acquaintance, came in to have a cup of coffee with her. As soon as the woman was seated at table she began to speak about Pustovalov—how good he was, what a steady man, and any woman could be glad to get him as a husband. Three days later Pustovalov himself paid Olenka a visit. He stayed only about ten minutes, and spoke little, but Olenka fell in love with him, fell in love so desperately that she did not sleep the whole night and burned as with fever. In the morning she sent for the elderly woman. Soon after, Olenka and Pustovalov were engaged, and the wedding followed.

Pustovalov and Olenka lived happily together. He usually stayed in the lumber-yard until dinner, then went out on business. In his absence Olenka took his place in the office until evening, attending to the book-keeping and despatching the orders.

"Lumber rises twenty per cent every year nowadays," she told her customers and acquaintances. "Imagine, we used to buy wood from our forests here. Now Vasichka has to go every year to the government of Mogilev to get wood. And what a tax!" she exclaimed, covering her cheeks with her hands in terror. "What a tax!"

She felt as if she had been dealing in lumber for ever so long, that the most important and essential thing in life was lumber. There was something touching and endearing in the way she pronounced the words, "beam," "joist," "plank," "stave," "lath," "gun-carriage," "clamp." At night she dreamed of whole mountains of boards and planks, long, endless rows of wagons conveying the wood somewhere, far, far from the city. She dreamed that a whole regiment of beams, 36 ft. x 5 in., were advancing in an upright position to do battle against the lumber-yard; that the beams and joists and clamps were knocking against each other, emitting the sharp crackling reports of dry wood, that they were all falling and then rising again, piling on top of each other. Olenka cried out in her sleep, and Pustovalov said to her gently:

"Olenka my dear, what is the matter? Cross yourself."

Her husband's opinions were all hers. If he thought the room was too hot, she thought so too. If he thought business was dull, she thought business was dull. Pustovalov was not fond of amusements and stayed home on holidays; she did the same.

"You are always either at home or in the office," said her friends.

"Why don't you go to the theatre or to the circus, darling?"

"Vasichka and I never go to the theatre," she answered sedately. "We have work to do, we have no time for nonsense. What does one get out of going to theatre?"

On Saturdays she and Pustovalov went to vespers, and on holidays to early mass. On returning home they walked side by side with rapt faces, an agreeable smell emanating from both of them and her silk dress rustling pleasantly. At home they drank tea with milk-bread and various jams, and then ate pie. Every day at noontime there was an appetising odour in the yard and outside the gate of cabbage soup, roast mutton, or duck; and, on fast days, of fish. You couldn't pass the gate without being seized by an acute desire to eat. The samovar was always boiling on the office table, and customers were treated to tea and biscuits. Once a week the married couple went to the baths and returned with red faces, walking side by side.

"We are getting along very well, thank God," said Olenka to her friends. "God grant that all should live as well as Vasichka and I."

When Pustovalov went to the government of Mogilev to buy wood, she was dreadfully homesick for him, did not sleep nights, and cried. Sometimes the veterinary surgeon of the regiment, Smirnov, a young man who lodged in the wing of her house, came to see her evenings. He related incidents, or they played cards together. This distracted her. The most interesting of his stories were those of his own life. He was married and had a son; but he had separated from his wife because she had deceived him, and now he hated her and sent her forty rubles a month for his son's support. Olenka sighed, shook her head, and was sorry for him.

"Well, the Lord keep you," she said, as she saw him off to the door by candlelight. "Thank you for coming to kill time with me. May God give you health. Mother in Heaven!" She spoke very sedately, very judiciously, imitating her husband. The veterinary surgeon had disappeared behind the door when she called out after him: "Do you know, Vladimir Platonych, you ought to make up with your wife. Forgive her, if only for the sake of your son. The child understands everything, you may be sure."

When Pustovalov returned, she told him in a low voice about the veterinary surgeon and his unhappy family life; and they sighed and shook their heads, and talked about the boy who must be homesick for his father. Then, by a strange association of ideas, they both stopped before the sacred images, made genuflections, and prayed to God to send them children.

And so the Pustovalovs lived for full six years, quietly and peaceably, in perfect love and harmony. But once in the winter Vasily Andreyich, after drinking some hot tea, went out into the lumber-yard without a hat on his head, caught a cold and took sick. He was treated by the best physicians, but the malady progressed, and he died after an illness of four months. Olenka was again left a widow.

"To whom have you left me, my darling?" she wailed after the funeral. "How shall I live now without you, wretched creature that I am. Pity me, good people, pity me, fatherless and motherless, all alone in the world!"

She went about dressed in black and weepers, and she gave up wearing hats and gloves for good. She hardly left the house except to go to church and to visit her husband's grave. She almost led the life of a nun.

It was not until six months had passed that she took off the weepers and opened her shutters. She began to go out occasionally in the morning to market with her cook.

But how she lived at home and what went on there, could only be surmised. It could be surmised from the fact that she was seen in her little garden drinking tea with the veterinarian while he read the paper out loud to her, and also from the fact that once on meeting an acquaintance at the post-office, she said to her:

"There is no proper veterinary inspection in our town. That is why there is so much disease. You constantly hear of people getting sick from the milk and becoming infected by the horses and cows. The health of domestic animals ought really to be looked after as much as that of human beings."

She repeated the veterinarian's words and held the same opinions as he about everything. It was plain that she could not exist a single year without an attachment, and she found her new happiness in the wing of her house. In any one else this would have been condemned; but no one could think ill of Olenka. Everything in her life was so transparent. She and the veterinary surgeon never spoke about the change in their relations. They tried, in fact, to conceal it, but unsuccessfully; for Olenka could have no secrets.

When the surgeon's colleagues from the regiment came to see him, she poured tea, and served the supper, and talked to them about the cattle plague, the foot and mouth disease, and the municipal slaughter houses. The surgeon was dreadfully embarrassed, and after the visitors had left, he caught her hand and hissed angrily:

"Didn't I ask you not to talk about what you don't understand? When we doctors discuss things, please don't mix in. It's getting to be a nuisance."

She looked at him in astonishment and alarm, and asked:

"But, Volodichka, what am I to talk about?"

And she threw her arms round his neck, with tears in her eyes, and begged him not to be angry. And they were both happy.

But their happiness was of short duration. The veterinary surgeon went away with his regiment to be gone for good, when it was transferred to some distant place almost as far as Siberia, and Olenka was left alone.

Now she was completely alone. Her father had long been dead, and his armchair lay in the attic covered with dust and minus one leg. She got thin and homely, and the people who met her on the street no longer looked at her as they had used to, nor smiled at her. Evidently her best years were over, past and gone, and a new, dubious life was to begin which it were better not to think about.

In the evening Olenka sat on the steps and heard the music playing and the rockets bursting in the Tivoli; but it no longer aroused any response in her. She looked listlessly into the yard, thought of nothing, wanted nothing, and when night came on, she went to bed and dreamed of nothing but the empty yard. She ate and drank as though by compulsion.

And what was worst of all, she no longer held any opinions. She saw and understood everything that went on around her, but she could not form an opinion about it. She knew of nothing to talk about. And how dreadful not to have opinions! For instance, you see a bottle, or you see that it is raining, or you see a muzhik riding by in a wagon. But what the bottle or the rain or the muzhik are for, or what the sense of them all is, you cannot tell—you cannot tell, not for a thousand rubles. In the days of Kukin and Pustovalov and then of the veterinary surgeon, Olenka had had an explanation for everything, and would have given her opinion freely no matter about what. But now there was the same emptiness in her heart and brain as in her yard. It was as galling and bitter as a taste of wormwood.

Gradually the town grew up all around. The Gypsy Road had become a street, and where the Tivoli and the lumber-yard had been, there were now houses and a row of side streets. How quickly time flies! Olenka's house turned gloomy, the roof rusty, the shed slanting. Dock and thistles overgrew the yard. Olenka herself had aged and grown homely. In the summer she sat on the steps, and her soul was empty and dreary and bitter. When she caught the breath of spring, or when the wind wafted the chime of the cathedral bells, a sudden flood of memories would pour over her, her heart would expand with a tender warmth, and the tears would stream down her cheeks. But that lasted only a moment. Then would come emptiness again, and the feeling, What is the use of living? The black kitten Bryska rubbed up against her and purred softly, but the little creature's caresses left Olenka untouched.

That was not what she needed. What she needed was a love that would absorb her whole being, her reason, her whole soul, that would give her ideas, an object in life, that would warm her aging blood. And she shook the black kitten off her skirt angrily, saying:

"Go away! What are you doing here?"

And so day after day, year after year not a single joy, not a single opinion. Whatever Marva, the cook, said was all right.

One hot day in July, towards evening, as the town cattle were being driven by, and the whole yard was filled with clouds of dust, there was suddenly a knocking at the gate. Olenka herself went to open it, and was dumbfounded to behold the veterinarian Smirnov. He had turned grey and was dressed as a civilian. All the old memories flooded into her soul, she could not restrain herself, she burst out crying, and laid her head on Smirnov's breast without saying a word. So overcome was she that she was totally unconscious of how they walked into the house and seated themselves to drink tea.

"My darling!" she murmured, trembling with

joy. "Vladimir Platonych, from where has God sent you?"

"I want to settle here for good," he told her. "I have resigned my position and have come here to try my fortune as a free man and lead a settled life. Besides, it's time to send my boy to the gymnasium. He is grown up now. You know, my wife and I have become reconciled."

"Where is she?" asked Olenka.

"At the hotel with the boy. I am looking for lodgings."

"Good gracious, bless you, take my house. Why won't my house do? Oh, dear! Why, I won't ask any rent of you," Olenka burst out in the greatest excitement, and began to cry again. "You live here, and the wing will be enough for me. Oh, Heavens, what a joy!"

The very next day the roof was being painted and the walls whitewashed, and Olenka, arms akimbo, was going about the yard superintending. Her face brightened with her old smile. Her whole being revived and freshened, as though she had awakened from a long sleep. The veterinarian's wife and child arrived. She was a thin, plain woman, with a crabbed expression. The boy Sasha, small for his ten years of age, was a chubby child, with clear blue eyes and dimples in his cheeks. He made for the kitten the instant he entered the yard, and the place rang with his happy laughter.

"Is that your cat, auntie?" he asked Olenka. "When she has little kitties, please give me one. Mamma is awfully afraid of mice."

Olenka chatted with him, gave him tea, and there was a sudden warmth in her bosom and a soft gripping at her heart, as though the boy were her own son.

In the evening, when he sat in the dining-room studying his lessons, she looked at him tenderly and whispered to herself:

"My darling, my pretty. You are such a clever child, so good to look at."

"An island is a tract of land entirely surrounded by water," he recited.

"An island is a tract of land," she repeated—the first idea asseverated with conviction after so many years of silence and mental emptiness.

She now had her opinions, and at supper discussed with Sasha's parents how difficult the studies had become for the children at the gymnasium, but how, after all, a classical education was better than a commercial course, because when you graduated from the gymnasium then the road was open to you for any career at all. If you chose to, you could become a doctor, or, if you wanted to, you could become an engineer.

Sasha began to go to the gymnasium. His mother left on a visit to her sister in Kharkov and never came back. The father was away every day inspecting cattle, and sometimes was gone three whole days at a time, so that Sasha, it seemed to Olenka, was utterly abandoned, was treated as if he were quite superfluous, and must be dying of hunger. So she transferred him into the wing along with herself and fixed up a little room for him there.

Every morning Olenka would come into his room and find him sound asleep with his hand tucked under his cheek, so quiet that he seemed not to be breathing. What a shame to have to wake him, she thought.

"Sashenka," she said sorrowingly, "get up, darling. It's time to go to the gymnasium."

He got up, dressed, said his prayers, then sat down to drink tea. He drank three glasses of tea, ate two large cracknels and half a buttered roll. The sleep was not yet out of him, so he was a little cross.

"You don't know your fable as you should, Sashenka," said Olenka, looking at him as though he were departing on a long journey. "What a lot of trouble you are. You must try hard and learn, dear, and mind your teachers."

"Oh, let me alone, please," said Sasha.

Then he went down the street to the gymnasium, a little fellow wearing a large cap and carrying a satchel on his back. Olenka followed him noiselessly.

"Sashenka," she called.

He looked round and she shoved a date or a caramel into his hand. When he reached the street of the gymnasium, he turned around and said, ashamed of being followed by a tall, stout woman:

"You had better go home, aunt. I can go the rest of the way myself."

She stopped and stared after him until he had disappeared into the school entrance.

Oh, how she loved him! Not one of her other ties had been so deep. Never before had she given herself so completely, so disinterestedly, so cheerfully as now that her maternal instincts were all aroused. For this boy, who was not hers, for the dimples in his cheeks and for his big cap, she would have given her life, given it with joy and with tears of rapture. Why? Ah, indeed, why?

When she had seen Sasha off to the gymnasium, she returned home quietly, content, serene, overflowing with love. Her face, which had grown younger in the last half year, smiled and beamed. People who met her were pleased as they looked at her.

"How are you, Olga Semyonovna, darling? How are you getting on, darling?"

"The gymnasium course is very hard nowadays," she told at the market. "It's no joke. Yesterday the first class had a fable to learn by heart, a Latin translation, and a problem. How is a little fellow to do all that?"

And she spoke of the teacher and the lessons and the text-books, repeating exactly what Sasha said about them.

At three o'clock they had dinner. In the evening they prepared the lessons together, and Olenka wept with Sasha over the difficulties. When she put him to bed, she lingered a long time making the sign of the cross over him and muttering a prayer. And when she lay in bed, she dreamed of the far-away, misty future when Sasha would finish his studies and become a doctor or an engineer, have a large house of his own, with horses and a carriage, marry and have children. She would fall asleep still thinking of the same things, and tears would roll down her cheeks from her closed eyes. And the black cat would lie at her side purring: "Mrr, mrr, mrr."

Suddenly there was a loud knocking at the gate. Olenka woke up breathless with fright, her heart beating violently. Half a minute later there was another knock.

"A telegram from Kharkov," she thought, her whole body in a tremble.

"His mother wants Sasha to come to her in Kharkov. Oh, great God!"

She was in despair. Her head, her feet, her hands turned cold. There was no unhappier creature in the world, she felt. But another minute passed, she heard voices. It was the veterinarian coming home from the club.

"Thank God," she thought. The load gradually fell from her heart, she was at ease again. And she went back to bed, thinking of Sasha who lay fast asleep in the next room and sometimes cried out in his sleep:

"I'll give it to you! Get away! Quit your scrapping!"

THE BET

BY ANTON P. CHEKHOV

I

It was a dark autumn night. The old banker was pacing from corner to corner of his study, recalling to his mind the party he gave in the autumn fifteen years before. There were many clever people at the party and much interesting conversation. They talked among other things of capital punishment. The guests, among them not a few scholars and journalists, for the most part disapproved of capital punishment. They found it obsolete as a means of punishment, unfitted to a Christian State and immoral. Some of them thought that capital punishment should be replaced universally by life-imprisonment.

"I don't agree with you," said the host. "I

myself have experienced neither capital punishment nor life-imprisonment, but if one may judge a priori, then in my opinion capital punishment is more moral and more humane than imprisonment. Execution kills instantly, life-imprisonment kills by degrees. Who is the more humane executioner, one who kills you in a few seconds or one who draws the life out of you incessantly, for years?"

"They're both equally immoral," remarked one of the guests, "because their purpose is the same, to take away life. The State is not God. It has no right to take away that which it cannot give back, if it should so desire."

Among the company was a lawyer, a young man of about twenty-five. On being asked his opinion, he said:

"Capital punishment and life-imprisonment are equally immoral; but if I were offered the choice between them, I would certainly choose the second. It's better to live somehow than not to live at all."

There ensued a lively discussion. The banker who was then younger and more nervous suddenly lost his temper, banged his fist on the table, and turning to the young lawyer, cried out:

"It's a lie. I bet you two millions you wouldn't stick in a cell even for five years."

"If you mean it seriously," replied the lawyer, "then I bet I'll stay not five but fifteen."

"Fifteen! Done!" cried the banker. "Gentlemen, I stake two millions."

"Agreed. You stake two millions, I my freedom," said the lawyer.

So this wild, ridiculous bet came to pass. The banker, who at that time had too many millions to count, spoiled and capricious, was beside himself with rapture. During supper he said to the lawyer jokingly:

"Come to your senses, young roan, before it's too late. Two millions are nothing to me, but you stand to lose three or four of the best years of your life. I say three or four, because you'll never stick it out any longer. Don't forget either, you unhappy man, that voluntary is much heavier than enforced imprisonment. The idea that you have the right to free yourself at any moment will poison the whole of your life in the cell. I pity you."

And now the banker, pacing from corner to corner, recalled all this and asked himself:

"Why did I make this bet? What's the good? The lawyer loses fifteen years of his life and I throw away two millions. Will it convince people that capital punishment is worse or better than imprisonment for life? No, no! all stuff and rubbish. On my part, it was the caprice of a well-fed man; on the lawyer's pure greed of gold."

He recollected further what happened after the evening party. It was decided that the lawyer must undergo his imprisonment under the strictest observation, in a garden wing of the banker's house. It was agreed that during the period he would be deprived of the right to cross the threshold, to see living people, to hear human voices, and to receive letters and newspapers. He was permitted to have a musical instrument, to read books, to write letters, to drink wine and smoke tobacco. By the agreement he could communicate, but only in silence, with the outside world through a little window specially constructed for this purpose.

Everything necessary, books, music, wine, he could receive in any quantity by sending a note through the window. The agreement provided for all the minutest details, which made the confinement strictly solitary, and it obliged the lawyer to remain exactly fifteen years from twelve o'clock of November 14th, 1870, to twelve o'clock of November 14th, 1885. The least attempt on his part to violate the conditions, to escape if only for two minutes before the time freed the banker from the obligation to pay him the two millions.

During the first year of imprisonment, the lawyer, as far as it was possible to judge from his short notes, suffered terribly from loneliness and boredom. From his wing day and night came the sound of the piano. He rejected wine and tobacco. "Wine," he wrote, "excites desires, and desires are the chief foes of a prisoner; besides, nothing is more boring than to drink good wine alone," and tobacco spoils the air in his room. During the first year the lawyer was sent books of a light character; novels with a complicated love interest, stories of crime and fantasy, comedies, and so on.

In the second year the piano was heard

no longer and the lawyer asked only for classics. In the fifth year, music was heard again, and the prisoner asked for wine. Those who watched him said that during the whole of that year he was only eating, drinking, and lying on his bed. He yawned often and talked angrily to himself. Books he did not read. Sometimes at nights he would sit down to write. He would write for a long time and tear it all up in the morning. More than once he was heard to weep.

In the second half of the sixth year, the prisoner began zealously to study languages, philosophy, and history. He fell on these subjects so hungrily that the banker hardly had time to get books enough for him. In the space of four years about six hundred volumes were bought at his request. It was while that passion lasted that the banker received the following letter from the prisoner: "My dear gaoler, I am writing these lines in six languages. Show them to experts. Let them read them. If they do not find one single mistake, I beg you to give orders to have a gun fired off in the garden. By the noise I shall know that my efforts have not been in vain. The geniuses of all ages and countries speak in different languages; but in them all burns the same flame. Oh, if you knew my heavenly happiness now that I can understand them!" The prisoner's desire was fulfilled. Two shots were fired in the garden by the banker's order.

Later on, after the tenth year, the lawyer sat immovable before his table and read only the New Testament. The banker found it strange that a man who in four years had mastered six hundred erudite volumes, should have spent nearly a year in reading one book, easy to understand and by no means thick. The New Testament was then replaced by the history of religions and theology.

During the last two years of his confinement the prisoner read an extraordinary amount, quite haphazard. Now he would apply himself to the natural sciences, then he would read Byron or Shakespeare. Notes used to come from him in which he asked to be sent at the same time a book on chemistry, a text-book of medicine, a novel, and some treatise on philosophy or theology. He read as though he were swimming in the sea among broken pieces of wreckage, and in his desire to save his life was eagerly grasping one piece after another.

II

The banker recalled all this, and thought:

"To-morrow at twelve o'clock he receives his freedom. Under the agreement, I shall have to pay him two millions. If I pay, it's all over with me. I am ruined for ever ..."

Fifteen years before he had too many millions to count, but now he was afraid to ask himself which he had more of, money or debts. Gambling on the Stock-Exchange, risky speculation, and the recklessness of which he could not rid himself even in old age, had gradually brought his business to decay; and the fearless, self-confident, proud man of business had become an ordinary banker, trembling at every rise and fall in the market.

"That cursed bet," murmured the old man clutching his head in despair... "Why didn't the man die? He's only forty years old. He will take away my last farthing, marry, enjoy life, gamble on the Exchange, and I will look on like an envious beggar and hear the same words from him every day: 'I'm obliged to you for the happiness of my life. Let me help you.' No, it's too much! The only escape from bankruptcy and disgrace—is that the man should die."

The clock had just struck three. The banker was listening. In the house every one was asleep, and one could hear only the frozen trees whining outside the windows. Trying to make no sound, he took out of his safe the key of the door which had not been opened for fifteen years, put on his overcoat, and went out of the house. The garden was dark and cold. It was raining. A damp, penetrating wind howled in the garden and gave the trees no rest. Though he strained his eyes, the banker could see neither the ground, nor the white statues, nor the garden wing, nor the trees. Approaching the garden wing, he called the watchman twice. There was no answer. Evidently the watchman had taken shelter from the bad weather and was now asleep somewhere in the kitchen or the greenhouse.

"If I have the courage to fulfil my intention," thought the old man, "the suspicion will fall on the watchman first of all."

In the darkness he groped for the steps and the door and entered the hall of the garden-wing, then poked his way into a narrow passage and struck a match. Not a soul was there. Some one's bed, with no bedclothes on it, stood there, and an iron stove loomed dark in the corner. The seals on the door that led into the prisoner's room were unbroken.

When the match went out, the old man, trembling from agitation, peeped into the little window.

In the prisoner's room a candle was burning dimly. The prisoner himself sat by the table. Only his back, the hair on his head and his hands were visible. Open books were strewn about on the table, the two chairs, and on the carpet near the table.

Five minutes passed and the prisoner never once stirred. Fifteen years' confinement had taught him to sit motionless. The banker tapped on the window with his finger, but the prisoner made no movement in reply. Then the banker cautiously tore the seals from the door and put the key into the lock. The rusty lock gave a hoarse groan and the door creaked. The banker expected instantly to hear a cry of surprise and the sound of steps. Three minutes passed and it was as quiet inside as it had been before. He made up his mind to enter.

Before the table sat a man, unlike an ordinary human being. It was a skeleton, with tight-drawn skin, with long curly hair like a woman's, and a shaggy beard. The colour of his face was yellow, of an earthy shade; the cheeks were sunken, the back long and narrow, and the hand upon which he leaned his hairy head was so lean and skinny that it was painful to look upon. His hair was already silvering with grey, and no one who glanced at the senile emaciation of the face would have believed that he was only forty years old. On the table, before his bended head, lay a sheet of paper on which something was written in a tiny hand.

"Poor devil," thought the banker, "he's asleep and probably seeing millions in his dreams. I have only to take and throw this half-dead thing on the bed, smother him a moment with the pillow, and the most careful examination will find no trace of unnatural death. But, first, let us read what he has written here."

The banker took the sheet from the table and read:

"To-morrow at twelve o'clock midnight, I shall obtain my freedom and the right to mix with people. But before I leave this room and see the sun I think it necessary to say a few words to you. On my own clear conscience and before God who sees me I declare to you that I despise freedom, life, health, and all that your books call the blessings of the world.

"For fifteen years I have diligently studied earthly life. True, I saw neither the earth nor the people, but in your books I drank fragrant wine, sang songs, hunted deer and wild boar in the forests, loved women... And beautiful women, like clouds ethereal, created by the magic of your poets' genius, visited me by night and whispered to me wonderful tales, which made my head drunken. In your books I climbed the summits of Elbruz and Mont Blanc and saw from there how the sun rose in the morning, and in the evening suffused the sky, the ocean and the mountain ridges with a purple gold. I saw from there how above me lightnings glimmered cleaving the clouds; I saw green forests, fields, rivers, lakes, cities; I heard syrens singing, and the playing of the pipes of Pan; I touched the wings of beautiful devils who came flying to me to speak of

God... In your books I cast myself into bottomless abysses, worked miracles, burned cities to the ground, preached new religions, conquered whole countries...

"Your books gave me wisdom. All that unwearying human thought created in the centuries is compressed to a little lump in my skull. I know that I am cleverer than you all.

"And I despise your books, despise all worldly blessings and wisdom. Everything is void, frail, visionary and delusive as a mirage. Though you be proud and wise and beautiful, yet will death wipe you from the face of the earth like the mice underground; and your posterity, your history, and the immortality of your men of genius will be as frozen slag, burnt down together with the terrestrial globe.

"You are mad, and gone the wrong way. You take falsehood for truth and ugliness for beauty. You would marvel if suddenly apple and orange trees should bear frogs and lizards instead of fruit, and if roses should begin to breathe the odour of a sweating horse. So do I marvel at you, who have bartered heaven for earth. I do not want to understand you.

"That I may show you in deed my contempt for that by which you live, I waive the two millions of which I once dreamed as of paradise, and which I now despise. That I may deprive myself of my right to them, I shall come out from here five minutes before the stipulated term, and thus shall violate the agreement."

When he had read, the banker put the sheet on the table, kissed the head of the strange man, and began to weep. He went out of the wing. Never at any other time, not even after his terrible losses on the Exchange, had he felt such contempt for himself as now. Coming home, he lay down on his bed, but agitation and tears kept him a long time from sleeping...

The next morning the poor watchman came running to him and told him that they had seen the man who lived in the wing climb through the window into the garden. He had gone to the gate and disappeared. The banker instantly went with his servants to the wing and established the escape of his prisoner. To avoid unnecessary rumours he took the paper with the renunciation from the table and, on his return, locked it in his safe.

VANKA

BY ANTON P. CHEKHOV

Nine-year-old Vanka Zhukov, who had been apprentice to the shoemaker Aliakhin for three months, did not go to bed the night before Christmas. He waited till the master and mistress and the assistants had gone out to an early church-service, to procure from his employer's cupboard a small phial of ink and a penholder with a rusty nib; then, spreading a crumpled sheet of paper in front of him, he began to write.

Before, however, deciding to make the first letter, he looked furtively at the door and at the window, glanced several times at the sombre ikon, on either side of which stretched shelves full of lasts, and heaved a heart-rending sigh. The sheet of paper was spread on a bench, and he himself was on his knees in front of it.

"Dear Grandfather Konstantin Makarych,"

he wrote, "I am writing you a letter. I wish you a Happy Christmas and all God's holy best. I have no mamma or papa, you are all I have."

Vanka gave a look towards the window in which shone the reflection of his candle, and vividly pictured to himself his grandfather, Konstantin Makarych, who was night-watchman at Messrs. Zhivarev. He was a small, lean, unusually lively and active old man of sixty-five, always smiling and blear-eyed. All day he slept in the servants' kitchen or trifled with the cooks. At night, enveloped in an ample sheep-skin coat, he strayed round the domain tapping with his cudgel. Behind him, each hanging its head, walked the old bitch Kashtanka, and the dog Viun, so named because of his black coat and long body and his resemblance to a loach. Viun was an unusually civil and friendly dog, looking as kindly at a stranger as at his masters, but he was not to be trusted. Beneath his deference and humbleness was hid the most inquisitorial maliciousness. No one knew better than he how to sneak up and take a bite at a leg, or slip into the larder or steal a muzhik's chicken. More than once they had nearly broken his hind-legs, twice he had been hung up, every week he was nearly flogged to death, but he always recovered.

At this moment, for certain, Vanka's grandfather must be standing at the gate, blinking his eyes at the bright red windows of the village church, stamping his feet in their high-felt boots, and jesting with the people in the yard; his cudgel will be hanging from his belt, he will be hugging himself with cold, giving a little dry, old man's cough, and at times pinching a servant-girl or a cook.

"Won't we take some snuff?" he asks, holding out his snuff-box to the women. The women take a pinch of snuff, and sneeze.

The old man goes into indescribable ecstasies, breaks into loud laughter, and cries:

"Off with it, it will freeze to your nose!"

He gives his snuff to the dogs, too. Kashtanka sneezes, twitches her nose, and walks away offended. Viun deferentially refuses to sniff and wags his tail. It is glorious weather, not a breath of wind, clear, and frosty; it is a dark night, but the whole village, its white roofs and streaks of smoke from the chimneys, the trees silvered with hoar-frost, and the snowdrifts, you can see it all. The sky scintillates with bright twinkling stars, and the Milky Way stands out so clearly that it looks as if it had been polished and rubbed over with snow for the holidays...

Vanka sighs, dips his pen in the ink, and continues to write:

"Last night I got a thrashing, my master dragged me by my hair into the yard, and belaboured me with a shoe-maker's stirrup, because, while I was rocking his brat in its cradle, I unfortunately fell asleep. And during the week, my mistress told me to clean a herring, and I began by its tail, so she took the herring and stuck its snout into my face. The assistants tease me, send me to the tavern for vodka, make me steal the master's cucumbers, and the master beats me with whatever is handy. Food there is none; in the morning it's bread, at dinner gruel, and in the evening bread again. As for tea or sour-cabbage soup, the master and the mistress themselves guzzle that. They make me sleep in the vestibule, and when their brat cries, I don't sleep at all, but have to rock the cradle. Dear Grandpapa, for Heaven's sake, take me away from here, home to our village, I can't bear this any more... I bow to the ground to you, and will pray to God for ever and ever, take me from here or I shall die..."

The corners of Vanka's mouth went down, he rubbed his eyes with his dirty fist, and sobbed.

"I'll grate your tobacco for you," he continued, "I'll pray to God for you, and if there is anything wrong, then flog me like the grey goat. And if you really think I shan't find work, then I'll ask the manager, for Christ's sake, to let me clean the boots, or I'll go instead of Fedya as underherdsman. Dear Grandpapa, I can't bear this any more, it'll kill me... I wanted to run away to our village, but I have no boots, and I was afraid of the frost, and when I grow up I'll look after you, no one shall harm you, and when you die I'll pray for the repose of your soul, just like I do for mamma Pelagueya.

"As for Moscow, it is a large town, there are all gentlemen's houses, lots of horses, no sheep, and the dogs are not vicious. The children don't come round at Christmas with a star, no one is allowed to sing in the choir, and once I saw in a shop window hooks on a line and fishing rods, all for sale, and for every kind of fish, awfully convenient. And there was one hook which would catch a sheat-fish weighing a pound. And there are shops with guns, like the master's, and I am sure they must cost 100 rubles each. And in the meat-shops there are woodcocks, partridges, and hares, but who shot them or where they come from, the shopman won't say.

"Dear Grandpapa, and when the masters give a Christmas tree, take a golden walnut and hide it in my green box. Ask the young lady, Olga Ignatyevna, for it, say it's for Vanka."

Vanka sighed convulsively, and again stared at the window. He remembered that his grandfather always went to the forest for the Christmas tree, and took his grandson with him. What happy times! The frost crackled, his grandfather crackled, and as they both did, Vanka did the same. Then before cutting down the Christmas tree his grandfather smoked his pipe, took a long pinch of snuff, and made fun of poor frozen little Vanka... The young fir trees, wrapt in hoar-frost, stood motionless, waiting for which of them would die. Suddenly a hare springing from somewhere would dart over the snowdrift... His grandfather could not help shouting:

"Catch it, catch it, catch it! Ah, short-tailed devil!"

When the tree was down, his grandfather dragged it to the master's house, and there they set about decorating it. The young lady, Olga Ignatyevna, Vanka's great friend, busied herself most about it. When little Vanka's mother, Pelagueya, was still alive, and was servant-woman in the house, Olga Ignatyevna used to stuff him with sugar-candy, and, having nothing to do, taught him to read, write, count up to one hundred, and even to dance the quadrille. When Pelagueya died, they placed the orphan Vanka in the kitchen with his grandfather, and from the kitchen he was sent to Moscow to Aliakhin, the shoemaker.

"Come quick, dear Grandpapa," continued Vanka, "I beseech you for Christ's sake take me from here. Have pity on a poor orphan, for here they beat me, and I am frightfully hungry, and so sad that I can't tell you, I cry all the time. The other day the master hit me on the head with a last; I fell to the ground, and only just returned to life. My life is a misfortune, worse than any dog's... I send greetings to Aliona, to one-eyed Tegor, and the coachman, and don't let any one have my mouth-organ. I remain, your grandson, Ivan Zhukov, dear Grandpapa, do come."

Vanka folded his sheet of paper in four, and put it into an envelope purchased the night before for a kopek. He thought a little, dipped the pen into the ink, and wrote the address:

"The village, to my grandfather." He then scratched his head, thought again, and added: "Konstantin Makarych." Pleased at not having been interfered with in his writing, he put on his cap, and, without putting on his sheep-skin coat, ran out in his shirt-sleeves into the street.

The shopman at the poulterer's, from whom he had inquired the night before, had told him that letters were to be put into post-boxes, and from there they were conveyed over the whole earth in mail troikas by drunken post-boys and to the sound of bells. Vanka ran to the first post-box and slipped his precious letter into the slit.

An hour afterwards, lulled by hope, he was sleeping soundly. In his dreams he saw a stove, by the stove his grandfather sitting with his legs dangling down, barefooted, and reading a letter to the cooks, and Viun walking round the stove wagging his tail.

ONE AUTUMN NIGHT

BY MAXIM GORKY

Once in the autumn I happened to be in a very unpleasant and inconvenient position. In the town where I had just arrived and where I knew not a soul, I found myself without a farthing in my pocket and without a night's lodging.

Having sold during the first few days every part of my costume without which it was still possible to go about, I passed from the town into the quarter called "Yste," where were the steamship wharves—a quarter which during the navigation season fermented with boisterous, laborious life, but now was silent and deserted, for we were in the last days of October.

Dragging my feet along the moist sand, and obstinately scrutinising it with the desire to discover in it any sort of fragment of food, I wandered alone among the deserted buildings and warehouses, and thought how good it would be to get a full meal.

In our present state of culture hunger of the mind is more quickly satisfied than hunger of the body. You wander about the streets, you are surrounded by buildings not bad-looking from the outside and—you may safely say it—not so badly furnished inside, and the sight of them may excite within you stimulating ideas about architecture, hygiene, and many other wise and high-flying subjects. You may meet warmly and neatly dressed folks—all very polite, and turning away from you tactfully, not wishing offensively to notice the lamentable fact of your existence. Well, well, the mind of a hungry man is always better nourished and healthier than the mind of the well-fed man; and there you have a situation from which you may draw a very ingenious conclusion in favour of the ill fed.

The evening was approaching, the rain was falling, and the wind blew violently from the north. It whistled in the empty booths and shops, blew into the plastered window-panes of the taverns, and whipped into foam the wavelets of the river which splashed noisily on the sandy shore, casting high their white crests, racing one after another into the dim distance, and leaping impetuously over one another's shoulders. It seemed as if the river felt the proximity of winter, and was running at random away from the fetters of ice which the north wind might well have flung upon her that very night. The sky was heavy and dark; down from it swept incessantly scarcely visible drops of rain, and the melancholy elegy in nature all around me was emphasised by a couple of battered and misshapen willow-trees and a boat, bottom upwards, that was fastened to their roots.

The overturned canoe with its battered keel and the miserable old trees rifled by the cold wind—everything around me was bankrupt, barren, and dead, and the sky flowed with undryable tears... Everything around was waste and gloomy ... it seemed as if everything were dead, leaving me alone among the living, and for me also a cold death waited.

I was then eighteen years old—a good time!

I walked and walked along the cold wet sand, making my chattering teeth warble in honour of cold and hunger, when suddenly, as I was carefully searching for something to eat behind one of the empty crates, I perceived behind it, crouching on the ground, a figure in woman's clothes dank with the rain and clinging fast to her stooping shoulders. Standing over her, I watched to see what she was doing. It appeared that she was digging a trench in the sand with her hands—digging away under one of the crates.

"Why are you doing that?" I asked, crouching down on my heels quite close to her.

She gave a little scream and was quickly on her legs again. Now that she stood there staring at me, with her wide-open grey eyes full of terror, I perceived that it was a girl of my own age, with a very pleasant face embellished unfortunately by three large blue marks. This spoilt her, although these blue marks had been distributed with a remarkable sense of proportion, one at a time, and all were of equal size—two under the eyes, and one a little bigger on the forehead just over the bridge of the nose. This symmetry was evidently the work of an artist well inured to the business of spoiling the human physiognomy.

The girl looked at me, and the terror in her eyes gradually died out... She shook the sand from her hands, adjusted her cotton head-gear, cowered down, and said:

"I suppose you too want something to eat? Dig away then! My hands are tired. Over there"—she nodded her head in the direction of a booth—"there is bread for certain ... and sausages too... That booth is still carrying on business."

I began to dig. She, after waiting a little and looking at me, sat down beside me and began to help me.

We worked in silence. I cannot say now whether I thought at that moment of the criminal code, of morality, of proprietorship, and all the other things about which, in the opinion of many experienced persons, one ought to think every moment of one's life. Wishing to keep as close to the truth as possible, I must confess that apparently I was so deeply engaged in digging under the crate that I completely forgot about everything else except this one thing: What could be inside that crate?

The evening drew on. The grey, mouldy,

cold fog grew thicker and thicker around us. The waves roared with a hollower sound than before, and the rain pattered down on the boards of that crate more loudly and more frequently. Somewhere or other the night-watchman began springing his rattle.

"Has it got a bottom or not?" softly inquired my assistant. I did not understand what she was talking about, and I kept silence.

"I say, has the crate got a bottom? If it has we shall try in vain to break into it. Here we are digging a trench, and we may, after all, come upon nothing but solid boards. How shall we take them off? Better smash the lock; it is a wretched lock."

Good ideas rarely visit the heads of women, but, as you see, they do visit them sometimes. I have always valued good ideas, and have always tried to utilise them as far as possible.

Having found the lock, I tugged at it and wrenched off the whole thing. My accomplice immediately stooped down and wriggled like a serpent into the gaping-open, four cornered cover of the crate whence she called to me approvingly, in a low tone:

"You're a brick!"

Nowadays a little crumb of praise from a woman is dearer to me than a whole dithyramb from a man, even though he be more eloquent than all the ancient and modern orators put together. Then, however, I was less amiably disposed than I am now, and, paying no attention to the compliment of my comrade, I asked her curtly and anxiously:

"Is there anything?"

In a monotonous tone she set about calculating our discoveries.

"A basketful of bottles—thick furs—a sunshade—an iron pail."

All this was uneatable. I felt that my hopes had vanished... But suddenly she exclaimed vivaciously:

"Aha! here it is!"

"What?"

"Bread ... a loaf ... it's only wet ... take it!"

A loaf flew to my feet and after it herself, my valiant comrade. I had already bitten off a morsel, stuffed it in my mouth, and was chewing it…

"Come, give me some too!… And we mustn't stay here… Where shall we go?" she looked inquiringly about on all sides… It was dark, wet, and boisterous.

"Look! there's an upset canoe yonder … let us go there."

"Let us go then!" And off we set, demolishing our booty as we went, and filling our mouths with large portions of it… The rain grew more violent, the river roared; from somewhere or other resounded a prolonged mocking whistle—just as if Someone great who feared nobody was whistling down all earthly institutions and along with them this horrid autumnal wind and us its heroes. This whistling made my heart throb painfully, in spite of which I greedily went on eating, and in this respect the girl, walking on my left hand, kept even pace with me.

"What do they call you?" I asked her—why

I know not.

"Natasha," she answered shortly, munching loudly.

I stared at her. My heart ached within me; and then I stared into the mist before me, and it seemed to me as if the inimical countenance of my Destiny was smiling at me enigmatically and coldly.

* * * * *

The rain scourged the timbers of the skiff incessantly, and its soft patter induced melancholy thoughts, and the wind whistled as it flew down into the boat's battered bottom through a rift, where some loose splinters of wood were rattling together—a disquieting and depressing sound. The waves of the river were splashing on the shore, and sounded so monotonous and hopeless, just as if they were telling something unbearably dull and heavy, which was boring them into utter disgust, something from which they wanted to run away and yet were obliged to talk about all the same. The sound of the rain blended with their splashing, and a long-drawn sigh seemed to be floating above the overturned skiff—the endless, labouring sigh of the earth, injured and exhausted by the eternal changes from the bright and warm summer to the cold misty and damp autumn. The wind blew continually over the desolate shore and the foaming river—blew and sang its melancholy songs...

Our position beneath the shelter of the skiff was utterly devoid of comfort; it was narrow and damp, tiny cold drops of rain dribbled through the damaged bottom; gusts of wind penetrated it. We sat in silence and shivered with cold. I remembered that I wanted to go to sleep. Natasha leaned her back against the hull of the boat and curled herself up into a tiny ball. Embracing her knees with her hands, and resting her chin upon them, she stared doggedly at the river with wide-open eyes; on the pale patch of her face they seemed immense, because of the blue marks below them. She never moved, and this immobility and silence—I felt it—gradually produced within me a terror of my neighbour. I wanted to talk to her, but I knew not how to begin.

It was she herself who spoke.

"What a cursed thing life is!" she exclaimed

plainly, abstractedly, and in a tone of deep conviction.

But this was no complaint. In these words there was too much of indifference for a complaint. This simple soul thought according to her understanding—thought and proceeded to form a certain conclusion which she expressed aloud, and which I could not confute for fear of contradicting myself. Therefore I was silent, and she, as if she had not noticed me, continued to sit there immovable.

"Even if we croaked ... what then...?" Natasha began again, this time quietly and reflectively, and still there was not one note of complaint in her words. It was plain that this person, in the course of her reflections on life, was regarding her own case, and had arrived at the conviction that in order to preserve herself from the mockeries of life, she was not in a position to do anything else but simply "croak"—to use her own expression.

The clearness of this line of thought was inexpressibly sad and painful to me, and I felt that if I kept silence any longer I was really bound to weep... And it would have been shameful to have done this before a woman, especially as she was not weeping herself. I resolved to speak to her.

"Who was it that knocked you about?" I asked. For the moment I could not think of anything more sensible or more delicate.

"Pashka did it all," she answered in a dull and level tone.

"And who is he?"

"My lover... He was a baker."

"Did he beat you often?"

"Whenever he was drunk he beat me... Often!"

And suddenly, turning towards me, she began to talk about herself, Pashka, and their mutual relations. He was a baker with red moustaches and played very well on the banjo. He came to see her and greatly pleased her, for he was a merry chap and wore nice clean clothes. He had a vest which cost fifteen rubles and boots with dress tops. For these reasons she had fallen in love with him, and he became her "creditor." And when he became her creditor he made it his business to take away from her the money which her other friends gave to her for bonbons, and, getting drunk on this money, he would fall to beating her; but that would have been nothing if he hadn't also begun to "run after" other girls before her very eyes.

"Now, wasn't that an insult? I am not worse than the others. Of course that meant that he was laughing at me, the blackguard. The day before yesterday I asked leave of my mistress to go out for a bit, went to him, and there I found Dimka sitting beside him drunk. And he, too, was half seas over. I said, 'You scoundrel, you!' And he gave me a thorough hiding. He kicked me and dragged me by the hair. But that was nothing to what came after. He spoiled everything I had on—left me just as I am now! How could I appear before my mistress? He spoiled everything ... my dress and my jacket too—it was quite a new one; I gave a fiver for it ... and tore my kerchief from my head... Oh, Lord! What will become of me now?" she suddenly whined in a lamentable overstrained voice.

The wind howled, and became ever colder and more boisterous... Again my teeth began to dance up and down, and she, huddled up to avoid the cold, pressed as closely to me as she could, so that I could see the gleam of her eyes through the darkness.

"What wretches all you men are! I'd burn you all in an oven; I'd cut you in pieces. If any one of you was dying I'd spit in his mouth, and not pity him a bit. Mean skunks! You wheedle and wheedle, you wag your tails like cringing dogs, and we fools give ourselves up to you, and it's all up with us! Immediately you trample us underfoot... Miserable loafers"

She cursed us up and down, but there was no vigour, no malice, no hatred of these "miserable loafers" in her cursing that I could hear. The tone of her language by no means corresponded with its subject-matter, for it was calm enough, and the gamut of her voice was terribly poor.

Yet all this made a stronger impression on me than the most eloquent and convincing pessimistic books and speeches, of which I had read a good many and which I still read to this day. And this, you see, was because the agony of a dying person is much more natural and violent than the most minute and picturesque descriptions of death.

I felt really wretched—more from cold than from the words of my neighbour. I groaned softly and ground my teeth.

Almost at the same moment I felt two little arms about me—one of them touched my neck and the other lay upon my face—and at the same time an anxious, gentle, friendly voice uttered the question:

"What ails you?"

I was ready to believe that some one else was asking me this and not Natasha, who had just declared that all men were scoundrels, and expressed a wish for their destruction. But she it was, and now she began speaking quickly, hurriedly.

"What ails you, eh? Are you cold? Are you frozen? Ah, what a one you are, sitting there so silent like a little owl! Why, you should have told me long ago that you were cold. Come ... lie on the ground ... stretch yourself out and I will lie ... there! How's that? Now put your arms round me?... tighter! How's that? You shall be warm very soon now... And then we'll lie back to back… The night will pass so quickly, see if it won't. I say … have you too been drinking?… Turned out of your place, eh?… It doesn't matter."

And she comforted me… She encouraged me.

May I be thrice accursed! What a world of irony was in this single fact for me! Just imagine! Here was I, seriously occupied at this very time with the destiny of humanity, thinking of the re-organisation of the social system, of political revolutions, reading all sorts of devilishly-wise books whose abysmal profundity was certainly unfathomable by their very authors—at this very time, I say, I was trying with all my might to make of myself "a potent active social force." It even seemed to me that I had partially accomplished my object; anyhow, at this time, in my ideas about myself, I had got so far as to recognise that I had an exclusive right to exist, that I had the necessary greatness to deserve to live my life, and that I was fully competent to play a great historical part therein. And a woman was now warming me with her body, a wretched, battered, hunted creature, who had no place and no value in life, and whom I had never thought of helping till she helped me herself, and whom I really would not have known how to help in any way even if the thought of it had occurred to me.

Ah! I was ready to think that all this was happening to me in a dream—in a disagreeable, an oppressive dream.

But, ugh! it was impossible for me to think that, for cold drops of rain were dripping down upon me, the woman was pressing close to me, her warm breath was fanning my face, and—despite a slight odor of vodka—it did me good. The wind howled and raged, the rain smote upon the skiff, the waves splashed, and both of us, embracing each other convulsively, nevertheless shivered with cold. All this was only too real, and I am certain that nobody ever dreamed such an oppressive and horrid dream as that reality.

But Natasha was talking all the time of something or other, talking kindly and sympathetically, as only women can talk. Beneath the influence of her voice and kindly words a little fire began to burn up within me, and something inside my heart thawed in consequence.

Then tears poured from my eyes like a hailstorm, washing away from my heart much that was evil, much that was stupid, much sorrow and dirt which had fastened upon it before that night. Natasha comforted me.

"Come, come, that will do, little one! Don't take on! That'll do! God will give you another chance ... you will right yourself and stand in your proper place again ... and it will be all right..."

And she kept kissing me ... many kisses did she give me ... burning kisses ... and all for nothing...

Those were the first kisses from a woman that had ever been bestowed upon me, and they were the best kisses too, for all the subsequent kisses cost me frightfully dear, and really gave me nothing at all in exchange.

"Come, don't take on so, funny one! I'll manage for you to-morrow if you cannot find a place." Her quiet persuasive whispering sounded in my ears as if it came through a dream...

There we lay till dawn…

And when the dawn came, we crept from behind the skiff and went into the town… Then we took friendly leave of each other and never met again, although for half a year I searched in every hole and corner for that kind Natasha, with whom I spent the autumn night just described.

If she be already dead—and well for her if it were so—may she rest in peace! And if she be alive … still I say "Peace to her soul!" And may the consciousness of her fall never enter her soul … for that would be a superfluous and fruitless suffering if life is to be lived…

HER LOVER

BY MAXIM GORKY

An acquaintance of mine once told me the following story.

When I was a student at Moscow I happened to live alongside one of those ladies whose repute is questionable. She was a Pole, and they called her Teresa. She was a tallish, powerfully-built brunette, with black, bushy eyebrows and a large coarse face as if carved out by a hatchet—the bestial gleam of her dark eyes, her thick bass voice, her cabman-like gait and her immense muscular vigour, worthy of a fishwife, inspired me with horror. I lived on the top flight and her garret was opposite to mine. I never left my door open when I knew her to be at home. But this, after all, was a very rare occurrence. Sometimes I chanced to meet her on the staircase or in the yard, and she would smile upon me with a smile which seemed to me to be sly and cynical. Occasionally, I saw her drunk, with bleary eyes, tousled hair, and a particularly hideous grin. On such occasions she would speak to me.

"How d'ye do, Mr. Student!" and her stupid laugh would still further intensify my loathing of her. I should have liked to have changed my quarters in order to have avoided such encounters and greetings; but my little chamber was a nice one, and there was such a wide view from the window, and it was always so quiet in the street below—so I endured.

And one morning I was sprawling on my couch, trying to find some sort of excuse for not attending my class, when the door opened, and the bass voice of Teresa the loathsome resounded from my threshold:

"Good health to you, Mr. Student!"

"What do you want?" I said. I saw that her face was confused and supplicatory… It was a very unusual sort of face for her.

"Sir! I want to beg a favour of you. Will you grant it me?"

I lay there silent, and thought to myself:

"Gracious!... Courage, my boy!"

"I want to send a letter home, that's what it is," she said; her voice was beseeching, soft, timid.

"Deuce take you!" I thought; but up I jumped, sat down at my table, took a sheet of paper, and said:

"Come here, sit down, and dictate!"

She came, sat down very gingerly on a chair, and looked at me with a guilty look.

"Well, to whom do you want to write?"

"To Boleslav Kashput, at the town of Sviept-ziana, on the Warsaw
Road..."
"Well, fire away!"

"My dear Boles ... my darling ... my faithful lover. May the Mother of God protect thee! Thou heart of gold, why hast thou not written for such a long time to thy sorrowing little dove, Teresa?"

I very nearly burst out laughing. "A sorrowing little dove!" more than five feet high, with fists a stone and more in weight, and as black a face as if the little dove had lived all its life in a chimney, and had never once washed itself! Restraining myself somehow, I asked:

"Who is this Bolest?"

"Boles, Mr. Student," she said, as if offended with me for blundering over the name, "he is Boles—my young man."

"Young man!"

"Why are you so surprised, sir? Cannot I, a girl, have a young man?"

She? A girl? Well!

"Oh, why not?" I said. "All things are possible. And has he been your young man long?"

"Six years."

"Oh, ho!" I thought. "Well, let us write your letter…"

And I tell you plainly that I would willingly have changed places with this Boles if his fair correspondent had been not Teresa but something less than she.

"I thank you most heartily, sir, for your kind services," said Teresa to me, with a curtsey. "Perhaps I can show you some service, eh?"

"No, I most humbly thank you all the same."

"Perhaps, sir, your shirts or your trousers may want a little mending?"

I felt that this mastodon in petticoats had made me grow quite red with shame, and I told her pretty sharply that I had no need whatever of her services.

She departed.

A week or two passed away. It was evening. I was sitting at my window whistling and thinking of some expedient for enabling me to get away from myself. I was bored; the weather was dirty. I didn't want to go out, and out of sheer ennui I began a course of self-analysis and reflection. This also was dull enough work, but I didn't care about doing anything else. Then the door opened. Heaven be praised! Some one came in.

"Oh, Mr. Student, you have no pressing business, I hope?"

It was Teresa. Humph!

"No. What is it?"

"I was going to ask you, sir, to write me another letter."

"Very well! To Boles, eh?"

"No, this time it is from him."

"Wha-at?"

"Stupid that I am! It is not for me, Mr. Student, I beg your pardon. It is for a friend of mine, that is to say, not a friend but an acquaintance—a man acquaintance. He has a sweetheart just like me here, Teresa. That's how it is. Will you, sir, write a letter to this Teresa?"

I looked at her—her face was troubled, her fingers were trembling. I was a bit fogged at first—and then I guessed how it was.

"Look here, my lady," I said, "there are no Boleses or Teresas at all, and you've been telling me a pack of lies. Don't you come sneaking about me any longer. I have no wish whatever to cultivate your acquaintance. Do you understand?"

And suddenly she grew strangely terrified and distraught; she began to shift from foot to foot without moving from the place, and spluttered comically, as if she wanted to say something and couldn't. I waited to see what would come of all this, and I saw and felt that, apparently, I had made a great mistake in suspecting her of wishing to draw me from the path of righteousness. It was evidently something very different.

"Mr. Student!" she began, and suddenly, waving her hand, she turned abruptly towards the door and went out. I remained with a very unpleasant feeling in my mind. I listened. Her door was flung violently to—plainly the poor wench was very angry... I thought it over, and resolved to go to her, and, inviting her to come in here, write everything she wanted.

I entered her apartment. I looked round. She was sitting at the table, leaning on her elbows, with her head in her hands.

"Listen to me," I said.

Now, whenever I come to this point in my story, I always feel horribly awkward and idiotic. Well, well!

"Listen to me," I said.

She leaped from her seat, came towards me with flashing eyes, and laying her hands on my shoulders, began to whisper, or rather to hum in her peculiar bass voice:

"Look you, now! It's like this. There's no Boles at all, and there's no Teresa either. But what's that to you? Is it a hard thing for you to draw your pen over paper? Eh? Ah, and you, too! Still such a little fair-haired boy! There's nobody at all, neither Boles, nor Teresa, only me. There you have it, and much good may it do you!"

"Pardon me!" said I, altogether flabbergasted by such a reception, "what is it all about? There's no Boles, you say?"

"No. So it is."

"And no Teresa either?"

"And no Teresa. I'm Teresa."

I didn't understand it at all. I fixed my eyes upon her, and tried to make out which of us was taking leave of his or her senses. But she went again to the table, searched about for something, came back to me, and said in an offended tone:

"If it was so hard for you to write to Boles, look, there's your letter, take it! Others will write for me."

I looked. In her hand was my letter to Boles. Phew!

"Listen, Teresa! What is the meaning of all this? Why must you get others to write for you when I have already written it, and you haven't sent it?"

"Sent it where?"

"Why, to this—Boles."

"There's no such person."

I absolutely did not understand it. There was nothing for me but to spit and go. Then she explained.

"What is it?" she said, still offended. "There's no such person, I tell you," and she extended her arms as if she herself did not understand why there should be no such person. "But I wanted him to be… Am I then not a human creature like the rest of them? Yes, yes, I know, I know, of course… Yet no harm was done to any one by my writing to him that I can see…"

"Pardon me—to whom?"

"To Boles, of course."

"But he doesn't exist."

"Alas! alas! But what if he doesn't? He doesn't exist, but he might! I write to him, and it looks as if he did exist. And Teresa—that's me, and he replies to me, and then I write to him again…"

I understood at last. And I felt so sick, so miserable, so ashamed, somehow. Alongside of me, not three yards away, lived a human creature who had nobody in the world to treat her kindly, affectionately, and this human being had invented a friend for herself!

"Look, now! you wrote me a letter to Boles, and I gave it to some one else to read it to me; and when they read it to me I listened and fancied that Boles was there. And I asked you to write me a letter from Boles to Teresa—that is to me. When they write such a letter for me, and read it to me, I feel quite sure that Boles is there. And life grows easier for me in consequence."

"Deuce take you for a blockhead!" said I to myself when I heard this.

And from thenceforth, regularly, twice a week, I wrote a letter to Boles, and an answer from Boles to Teresa. I wrote those answers well... She, of course, listened to them, and wept like anything, roared, I should say, with her bass voice. And in return for my thus moving her to tears by real letters from the imaginary Boles, she began to mend the holes I had in my socks, shirts, and other articles of clothing. Subsequently, about three months after this history began, they put her in prison for something or other. No doubt by this time she is dead.

My acquaintance shook the ash from his cigarette, looked pensively up at the sky, and thus concluded:

Well, well, the more a human creature has tasted of bitter things the more it hungers after the sweet things of life. And we, wrapped round in the rags of our virtues, and regarding others through the mist of our self-sufficiency, and persuaded of our universal impeccability, do not understand this.

And the whole thing turns out pretty stupidly—and very cruelly. The fallen classes, we say. And who are the fallen classes, I should like to know? They are, first of all, people with the same bones, flesh, and blood and nerves as ourselves. We have been told this day after day for ages. And we actually listen—and the devil only knows how hideous the whole thing is. Or are we completely depraved by the loud sermonising of humanism? In reality, we also are fallen folks, and, so far as I can see, very deeply fallen into the abyss of self-sufficiency and the conviction of our own superiority. But enough of this. It is all as old as the hills—so old that it is a shame to speak of it. Very old indeed—yes, that's what it is!

THE DISTRICT DOCTOR

BY IVAN S. TURGENEV

One day in autumn on my way back from a remote part of the country I caught cold and fell ill. Fortunately the fever attacked me in the district town at the inn; I sent for the doctor. In half-an-hour the district doctor appeared, a thin, dark-haired man of middle height. He prescribed me the usual sudorific, ordered a mustard-plaster to be put on, very deftly slid a five-ruble note up his sleeve, coughing drily and looking away as he did so, and then was getting up to go home, but somehow fell into talk and remained. I was exhausted with feverishness; I foresaw a sleepless night, and was glad of a little chat with a pleasant companion. Tea was served. My doctor began to converse freely. He was a sensible fellow, and expressed himself with vigour and some humour. Queer things happen in the world: you may live a long while with some people, and be on friendly terms with them, and never once speak openly with them from your soul; with others you have scarcely time to get acquainted, and all at once you are pouring out to him—or he to you—all your secrets, as though you were at confession. I don't know how I gained the confidence of my new friend—anyway, with nothing to lead up to it, he told me a rather curious incident; and here I will report his tale for the information of the indulgent reader. I will try to tell it in the doctor's own words.

"You don't happen to know," he began in a weak and quavering voice (the common result of the use of unmixed Berezov snuff); "you don't happen to know the judge here, Mylov, Pavel Lukich?... You don't know him?... Well, it's all the same." (He cleared his throat and rubbed his eyes.) "Well, you see, the thing happened, to tell you exactly without mistake, in Lent, at the very time of the thaws. I was sitting at his house—our judge's, you know—playing preference. Our judge is a good fellow, and fond of playing preference. Suddenly" (the doctor made frequent use of this word, suddenly) "they tell me, 'There's a servant asking for you.' I say, 'What does he want?' They say, He has brought a note—it must be from a patient.' 'Give me the note,' I say. So it is from a patient—well and good—you understand—it's our bread and butter... But this is how it was: a lady, a widow, writes to me; she says, 'My daughter is dying. Come, for God's sake!' she says, 'and the horses have been sent for you.'... Well, that's all right. But she was twenty miles from the town, and it was midnight out of doors, and the roads in such a state, my word! And as she was poor herself, one could not expect more than two silver rubles, and even that problematic; and perhaps it might only be a matter of a roll of linen and a sack of oatmeal in payment. However, duty, you know, before everything: a fellow-creature may be dying. I hand over my cards at once to Kalliopin, the member of the provincial commission, and return home. I look; a wretched little trap was standing at the steps, with peasant's horses, fat—too fat—and their coat as shaggy as felt; and the coachman sitting with his cap off out of respect. Well, I think to myself, 'It's clear, my friend, these patients aren't rolling in riches.'... You smile; but I tell you, a poor man like me has to take everything into consideration... If the coachman sits like a prince, and doesn't touch his cap, and even sneers at you behind his beard, and flicks his whip—then you may bet on six rubles. But this case, I saw, had a very different air. However, I think there's no help for it; duty before everything. I snatch up the most necessary drugs, and set off. Will you believe it? I only just managed to get there at all. The road was infernal: streams, snow, watercourses, and the dyke had suddenly burst there—that was the worst of it! However, I arrived at last. It was a little thatched house. There was a light in the windows; that meant they expected me. I was met by an old lady, very venerable, in a cap. 'Save her!' she says; 'she is dying.' I say, 'Pray don't distress yourself—Where is the invalid?' 'Come this way.' I see a clean little room, a lamp in the corner; on the bed a girl of twenty, unconscious. She was in a burning heat, and breathing heavily—it was fever. There were two other girls, her sisters, scared and in tears. 'Yesterday,' they tell me, 'she was perfectly well and had a good appetite; this morning she complained of her head, and this evening, suddenly, you see, like this.' I say again: 'Pray don't be uneasy.' It's a doctor's duty, you know—and I went up to her and bled her, told them to put on a mustard-plaster, and prescribed a mixture. Meantime I looked at her; I looked at her, you know—there, by God! I had never seen such a face!—she was a beauty, in a word! I felt quite shaken with pity. Such lovely features; such eyes!... But, thank God! she became easier; she fell into a perspiration, seemed to come to her senses, looked round, smiled, and passed her hand over her face... Her sisters bent over her. They ask, 'How are you?' 'All right,' she says, and turns away. I looked at her; she had fallen asleep. 'Well,' I say, 'now the patient should be left alone.' So we all went out on tiptoe; only a maid remained, in case she was wanted. In the parlour there was a samovar standing on the table, and a bottle of rum; in our profession one can't get on without it. They gave me tea; asked me to stop the night... I consented: where could I go, indeed, at that time of night? The old lady kept groaning. 'What is it?' I say; 'she will live; don't worry yourself; you had better take a little rest yourself; it is about two o'clock.' 'But will you send to wake me if anything happens?' 'Yes, yes.' The old lady went away, and the girls too went to their own room; they made up a bed for me in the parlour. Well, I went to bed—but I could not get to sleep, for a wonder! for in reality I was very tired. I could not get my patient out of my head. At last I could not put up with it any longer; I got up suddenly; I think to myself, 'I will go and see how the patient is getting on.' Her bedroom was next to the parlour. Well, I got up, and gently opened the door—how my heart beat! I looked in: the servant was asleep, her mouth wide open, and even snoring, the wretch! but the patient lay with her face towards me and her arms flung wide apart, poor girl! I went up to her … when suddenly she opened her eyes and stared at me! 'Who is it? who is it?' I was in confusion. 'Don't be alarmed, madam,' I say; 'I am the doctor; I have come to see how you feel.' 'You the doctor?' 'Yes, the doctor; your mother sent for me from the town; we have bled you, madam; now pray go to sleep, and in a day or two, please God! we will set you on your feet again.' 'Ah, yes, yes, doctor, don't let me die… please, please.' 'Why do you talk like that? God bless you!' She is in a fever again, I think to myself; I felt her pulse; yes, she was feverish. She looked at me, and then took me by the hand. 'I will tell you why I don't want to die: I will tell you… Now we are alone; and only, please don't you … not to any one … Listen…' I bent down; she moved her lips quite to my ear; she touched my cheek with her hair—I confess my head went round—and began to whisper… I could make out nothing of it… Ah, she was delirious! … She whispered and whispered, but so quickly, and as if it were not in Russian; at last she finished, and shivering dropped her head on the pillow, and threatened me with her finger: 'Remember, doctor, to no one.' I calmed her somehow, gave her something to drink, waked the servant, and went away."

At this point the doctor again took snuff with exasperated energy, and for a moment seemed stupefied by its effects.

"However," he continued, "the next day, contrary to my expectations, the patient was no better. I thought and thought, and suddenly decided to remain there, even though my other patients were expecting me… And you know one can't afford to disregard that; one's practice suffers if one does. But, in the first place, the patient was really in danger; and secondly, to tell the truth, I felt strongly drawn to her. Besides, I liked the whole family. Though they were really badly off, they were singularly, I may say, cultivated people… Their father had been a learned man, an author; he died, of course, in poverty, but he had managed before he died to give his children an excellent education; he left a lot of books too. Either because I looked after the invalid very carefully, or for some other reason; anyway, I can venture to say all the household loved me as if I were one of the family... Meantime the roads were in a worse state than ever; all communications, so to say, were cut off completely; even medicine could with difficulty be got from the town... The sick girl was not getting better... Day after day, and day after day ... but ... here..." (The doctor made a brief pause.) "I declare I don't know how to tell you."... (He again took snuff, coughed, and swallowed a little tea.) "I will tell you without beating about the bush. My patient ... how should I say?... Well she had fallen in love with me ... or, no, it was not that she was in love ... however ... really, how should one say?" (The doctor looked down and grew red.) "No," he went on quickly, "in love, indeed! A man should not over-estimate himself. She was an educated girl, clever and well-read, and I had even forgotten my Latin, one may say, completely. As to appearance" (the doctor looked himself over with a smile) "I am nothing to boast of there either. But God Almighty did not make me a fool; I don't take black for white; I know a thing or two; I could see very clearly, for instance that Aleksandra Andreyevna—that was her name—did not feel love for me, but had a friendly, so to say, inclination—a respect or something for me. Though she herself perhaps mistook this sentiment, anyway this was her attitude; you may form your own judgment of it. But," added the doctor, who had brought out all these disconnected sentences without taking breath, and with obvious embarrassment, "I seem to be wandering rather—you won't understand anything like this ... There, with your leave, I will relate it all in order."

He drank off a glass of tea, and began in a calmer voice.

"Well, then. My patient kept getting worse and worse. You are not a doctor, my good sir; you cannot understand what passes in a poor fellow's heart, especially at first, when he begins to suspect that the disease is getting the upper hand of him. What becomes of his belief in himself? You suddenly grow so timid; it's indescribable. You fancy then that you have forgotten everything you knew, and that the patient has no faith in you, and that other people begin to notice how distracted you are, and tell you the symptoms with reluctance; that they are looking at you suspiciously, whispering... Ah! it's horrid! There must be a remedy, you think, for this disease, if one could find it. Isn't this it? You try—no, that's not it! You don't allow the medicine the necessary time to do good... You clutch at one thing, then at another. Sometimes you take up a book of medical prescriptions—here it is, you think! Sometimes, by Jove, you pick one out by chance, thinking to leave it to fate... But meantime a fellow-creature's dying, and another doctor would have saved him. 'We must have a consultation,' you say; 'I will not take the responsibility on myself.' And what a fool you look at such times! Well, in time you learn to bear it; it's nothing to you. A man has died—but it's not your fault; you treated him by the rules. But what's still more torture to you is to see blind faith in you, and to feel yourself that you are not able to be of use. Well, it was just this blind faith that the whole of Aleksandra Andreyevna's family had in me; they had forgotten to think that their daughter was in danger. I, too, on my side assure them that it's nothing, but meantime my heart sinks into my boots. To add to our troubles, the roads were in such a state that the coachman was gone for whole days together to get medicine. And I never left the patient's room; I could not tear myself away; I tell her amusing stories, you know, and play cards with her. I watch by her side at night. The old mother thanks me with tears in her eyes; but I think to myself, 'I don't deserve your gratitude.' I frankly confess to you—there is no object in concealing it now—I was in love with my patient. And Aleksandra Andreyevna had grown fond of me; she would not sometimes let any one be in her room but me. She began to talk to me, to ask me questions; where I had studied, how I lived, who are my people, whom I go to see. I feel that she ought not to talk; but to forbid her to—to forbid her resolutely, you know—I could not. Sometimes I held my head in my hands, and asked myself, "What are you doing, villain?"… And she would take my hand and hold it, give me a long, long look, and turn away, sigh, and say, 'How good you are!' Her hands were so feverish, her eyes so large and languid… 'Yes,' she says, 'you are a good, kind man; you are not like our neighbours… No, you are not like that… Why did I not know you till now!' 'Aleksandra Andreyevna, calm yourself,' I say… 'I feel, believe me, I don't know how I have gained … but there, calm yourself… All will be right; you will be well again.' And meanwhile I must tell you," continued the doctor, bending forward and raising his eyebrows, "that they associated very little with the neighbours, because the smaller people were not on their level, and pride hindered them from being friendly with the rich. I tell you, they were an exceptionally cultivated family; so you know it was gratifying for me. She would only take her medicine from my hands ... she would lift herself up, poor girl, with my aid, take it, and gaze at me... My heart felt as if it were bursting. And meanwhile she was growing worse and worse, worse and worse, all the time; she will die, I think to myself; she must die. Believe me, I would sooner have gone to the grave myself; and here were her mother and sisters watching me, looking into my eyes ... and their faith in me was wearing away. 'Well? how is she?' 'Oh, all right, all right!' All right, indeed! My mind was failing me. Well, I was sitting one night alone again by my patient. The maid was sitting there too, and snoring away in full swing; I can't find fault with the poor girl, though; she was worn out too. Aleksandra Andreyevna had felt very unwell all the evening; she was very feverish. Until midnight she kept tossing about; at last she seemed to fall asleep; at least, she lay still without stirring. The lamp was burning in the corner before the holy image. I sat there, you know, with my head bent; I even dozed a little. Suddenly it seemed as though some one touched me in the side; I turned round... Good God! Aleksandra Andreyevna was gazing with intent eyes at me ... her lips parted, her cheeks seemed burning. 'What is it?' 'Doctor, shall I die?' 'Merciful Heavens!' 'No, doctor, no; please don't tell me I shall live ... don't say so... If you knew... Listen! for God's sake don't conceal my real position,' and her breath came so fast. 'If I can know for certain that I must die ... then I will tell you all— all!' 'Aleksandra Andreyevna, I beg!' 'Listen; I have not been asleep at all ... I have been looking at you a long while... For God's sake!... I believe in you; you are a good man, an honest man; I entreat you by all that is sacred in the world—tell me the truth! If you knew how important it is for me... Doctor, for God's sake tell me... Am I in danger?' 'What can I tell you, Aleksandra Andreyevna, pray?' 'For God's sake, I beseech you!' 'I can't disguise from you,' I say, 'Aleksandra Andreyevna; you are certainly in danger; but God is merciful.' 'I shall die, I shall die.' And it seemed as though she were pleased; her face grew so bright; I was alarmed. 'Don't be afraid, don't be afraid! I am not frightened of death at all.' She suddenly sat up and leaned on her elbow. 'Now ... yes, now I can tell you that I thank you with my whole heart ... that you are kind and good—that I love you!' I stare at her, like one possessed; it was terrible for me, you know. 'Do you hear, I love you!' 'Aleksandra

Andreyevna, how have I deserved—' 'No, no, you don't—you don't understand me.'... And suddenly she stretched out her arms, and taking my head in her hands, she kissed it... Believe me, I almost screamed aloud... I threw myself on my knees, and buried my head in the pillow. She did not speak; her fingers trembled in my hair; I listen; she is weeping. I began to soothe her, to assure her... I really don't know what I did say to her. 'You will wake up the girl,' I say to her; 'Aleksandra Andreyevna, I thank you ... believe me ... calm yourself.' 'Enough, enough!' she persisted; 'never mind all of them; let them wake, then; let them come in—it does not matter; I am dying, you see... And what do you fear? why are you afraid? Lift up your head... Or, perhaps, you don't love me; perhaps I am wrong... In that case, forgive me.' 'Aleksandra Andreyevna, what are you saying!... I love you, Aleksandra Andreyevna.' She looked straight into my eyes, and opened her arms wide. 'Then take me in your arms.' I tell you frankly, I don't know how it was I did not go mad that night. I feel that my patient is killing herself; I see that she is not fully herself; I understand, too, that if she did not consider herself on the point of death, she would never have thought of me; and, indeed, say what you will, it's hard to die at twenty without having known love; this was what was torturing her; this was why, in despair, she caught at me—do you understand now? But she held me in her arms, and would not let me go. 'Have pity on me, Aleksandra Andreyevna, and have pity on yourself,' I say. 'Why,' she says; 'what is there to think of? You know I must die.' … This she repeated incessantly … 'If I knew that I should return to life, and be a proper young lady again, I should be ashamed … of course, ashamed … but why now?' 'But who has said you will die?' 'Oh, no, leave off! you will not deceive me; you don't know how to lie—look at your face.' … 'You shall live, Aleksandra Andreyevna; I will cure you; we will ask your mother's blessing … we will be united—we will be happy.' 'No, no, I have your word; I must die … you have promised me … you have told me.' … It was cruel for me—cruel for many reasons. And see what trifling things can do sometimes; it seems nothing at all, but it's painful. It occurred to her to ask me, what is my name; not my surname, but my first name. I must needs be so unlucky as to be called Trifon. Yes, indeed; Trifon Ivanich. Every one in the house called me doctor. However, there's no help for it. I say, 'Trifon, madam.' She frowned, shook her head, and muttered something in French—ah, something unpleasant, of course!—and then she laughed—disagreeably too. Well, I spent the whole night with her in this way. Before morning I went away, feeling as though I were mad. When I went again into her room it was daytime, after morning tea. Good God! I could scarcely recognise her; people are laid in their grave looking better than that. I swear to you, on my honour, I don't understand—I absolutely don't understand—now, how I lived through that experience. Three days and nights my patient still lingered on. And what nights! What things she said to me! And on the last night—only imagine to yourself—I was sitting near her, and kept praying to God for one thing only: 'Take her,' I said, 'quickly, and me with her.' Suddenly the old mother comes unexpectedly into the room. I had already the evening before told her—-the mother—there was little hope, and it would be well to send for a priest. When the sick girl saw her mother she said: 'It's very well you have come; look at us, we love one another—we have given each other our word.' 'What does she say, doctor? what does she say?' I turned livid. 'She is wandering,' I say; 'the fever.' But she: 'Hush, hush; you told me something quite different just now, and have taken my ring. Why do you pretend? My mother is good—she will forgive—she will understand—and I am dying. ... I have no need to tell lies; give me your hand.' I jumped up and ran out of the room. The old lady, of course, guessed how it was.

"I will not, however, weary you any longer, and to me too, of course, it's painful to recall all this. My patient passed away the next day. God rest her soul!" the doctor added, speaking quickly and with a sigh. "Before her death she asked her family to go out and leave me alone with her."

"'Forgive me,' she said; 'I am perhaps to blame towards you ... my illness ... but believe me, I have loved no one more than you ... do not forget me ... keep my ring.'"

The doctor turned away; I took his hand.

"Ah!" he said, "let us talk of something else, or would you care to play preference for a small stake? It is not for people like me to give way to exalted emotions. There's only one thing for me to think of; how to keep the children from crying and the wife from scolding. Since then, you know, I have had time to enter into lawful wedlock, as they say… Oh … I took a merchant's daughter—seven thousand for her dowry. Her name's Akulina; it goes well with Trifon. She is an ill-tempered woman, I must tell you, but luckily she's asleep all day… Well, shall it be preference?"

We sat down to preference for halfpenny points. Trifon Ivanich won two rubles and a half from me, and went home late, well pleased with his success.

Other Large Print Titles

The Wonder Book of Bible Stories is an ***illustrated*** collection of Bible stories from both Old and New Testament written mainly for the youth, but can be enjoyed by all age groups. This book is not meant to replace the Bible but functions as a appetizer.

8.5" x 11" (21.59 x 27.94 cm)
Black & White on White paper
188 pages
ISBN-13: 978-1541389113
ISBN-10: 1541389115

Visit us on
www.bigfontbooks.com

www.ingramcontent.com/pod-product-compliance
Lightning Source LLC
Chambersburg PA
CBHW070632310726
48982CB00001B/266

* 9 7 8 1 9 4 0 8 4 9 4 9 2 *